THE DOCTOR'S TWINS

LYDIA HALL

ALSO BY LYDIA HALL

BLURB

A crazy nightmare led me into the arms of a hot doctor that saved my life.

My abusive ex-husband was a bigger danger than I'd thought.

Escaping him was my only option but I'd already lost the baby growing inside me.

Ben was not only my gynecologist, he was also the man that gave me hope.

His touch soothed my pain, melting me instantly.

It made me forget that I'd escaped a dangerous criminal.

Ben was ex-military and he made me feel safe, but I'd already decided to protect my heart.

There was no way I was going to fall for my doctor.

He was way older than me and I had already been shattered by more bad news.

I'd never be able to carry a child again.

But Ben was the kind of man that could transform nightmares into miracles.

Maybe even *two* little miracles this time.

PEYTON TAYLOR

"Here's to freedom!" Alyssa shouted above the noise of the crowd and held up her shot glass filled with amber-colored tequila.

"No more cramming for exams!" I chimed in with a grin before I drained my shot glass and slammed it down on the table.

"Wow! This is good stuff," she said, cleared her throat, and sucked on a lemon wedge.

"Yeah, we better enjoy it. I reckon we won't be having too many more parties once our residency begins. Not if we're planning on saving lives anyway."

"True dat, sista."

Alyssa and I had officially passed our medical degree. Four years of late-night-cramming sessions and pep talks got us there in the end. Now, we were a mere four years away from the coveted prize— parking wherever we bloody well-liked! And answering to the title of Doctor so and so, of course.

"To you, Dr. Taylor," Alyssa winked and poured another shot.

"And you, Dr. Collins."

"Don't look now, but there are two insanely hot guys looking our way. The one with the sandy hair has been staring at you all night," Alyssa smirked.

My best friend and I were in Mexico for a week of well-deserved sun and fun before we tackled the next phase of our careers head-on. I was thoroughly enjoying the beaches and party atmosphere of Cancun, and judging by the crowd we were in, so were thousands of other visitors.

"Please, I'm way ahead of you," I smiled. "I noticed them ogling us ages ago."

"Ooh, don't look now. They're coming over," Alyssa remarked and switched to her game face.

A handsome man with dark eyes, and wavy, blondish hair looked directly at me before he spoke in a thick local accent. Yummy...Spanish...

"Hi. I'm Mateo."

He didn't seem to notice Alyssa but rather spoke to me as if I were the only woman in a club teeming with partygoers.

"Hi, Mateo," I said, not introducing myself just yet.

I was in a playful mood. Mr. Spanish Deliciousness was going to have to work for it.

"Hi, I'm Gabriel," the other looker introduced himself to Alyssa. "May we buy you ladies, a drink?"

Mateo's eyes didn't leave mine for a second. From what I could tell, Mateo must have had some success with his approach to meeting women, because he exhibited no shortage of confidence.

"Sure," Alyssa answered, nonchalantly. "I'm Alyssa and this is Peyton."

"Peyton," Mateo smiled. "American?"

"Uh-huh," I said and nodded.

"What would you like to drink, Peyton from America?" he asked me, completely ignoring Alyssa, who wasn't too offended as she seemed satisfied with Gabriel's attention.

"What would you suggest? Being a local and all."

"Patron En Lalique, of course," he said. "If you're going to get a feel for my country, you'd better sample one of our finest tequilas."

Hhmm, a man of means—and taste. Not that I was a snob, but the riff-raff held no allure for me. I wasn't one of those women who insisted on dating bad boys. All they brought was trouble.

"I'll take your word for it."

Alyssa and Gabriel headed for the dancefloor, while Mateo and I braved our way through the crowd to the bar. My handsome acquaintance was kind enough to lead the way and I was happy to check out his fine ass as he walked. Mateo was wearing cream, chino shorts, and a white, button-down, cotton shirt, both of which accentuated his flawless, olive skin.

Before long he held a bottle of golden liquid in one hand and two shot glasses in the other. I followed him to a table outside the club where it was less chaotic. He placed the tequila and two glasses down before pulling out the chair for me.

"Thank you," I said and sat down.

That was another point in his favor—not that I was keeping score.

"What brings you to Cancun, Peyton?"

"Alyssa and I are celebrating."

"Well, you certainly chose the right place for it. What are you celebrating, if you don't mind me asking?"

"She and I have just graduated from medical school."

"Brainy and beautiful. Congratulations."

"Thank you. What do you do, Mateo?" I just loved the way his name rolled off my tongue.

I wasn't going to openly gush at his compliment. However, his dark eyes and sexy smile did make something inside my stomach flutter. I couldn't put my finger on it, but there was something unusual about the man who'd spent a small fortune on the bottle of tequila he was now pouring from.

"I'm an investment banker."

"Sounds exciting. Here in Cancun?"

"No, in Mexico City. Have you been there yet?"

"I have not."

"Perhaps I could show you around. You haven't been to Mexico, strictly speaking, that is, until you've seen our spectacular capital."

Boy, this guy didn't dick around when it came to going after the object of his desire. It was nice being pursued by a man for a change. The guys back home were the same age as Alyssa and me and what most of them possessed in brain matter, they seemed to lack in balls. Boys, all boys.

Okay, the accent was a turn-on, too.

"I may take you up on that offer," I said and took a sip of tequila.

Alyssa and Gabriel emerged from the club, laughing and chatting.

"Gabriel and I are heading to a private party. A friend of ours has a place on the beach. Would you and Alyssa like to join us, Peyton?" Mateo asked.

I looked across at Alyssa before I answered. Her face told me everything I needed to know.

"Sure. Sounds like fun."

"Yeah, I think I've had enough of this rowdy crowd for one night," Alyssa said and inhaled a shot of tequila.

"Great," Gabriel smiled and took Alyssa by the hand.

"Ready?" Mateo asked me.

"Ready."

* * *

I was more than a little impressed with Mateo's friend's *place* on the beach. It was a luxury villa with spectacular views and an impressive art collection. I realized that I'd stepped into the world of beautiful people as soon as we arrived.

About fifty people were milling around. Mateo introduced me to the owner of the home, who I judged to be in his late thirties, or early forties. He greeted me warmly and insisted that Alyssa and I make ourselves at home.

"It's nice to meet you, Adam. Do I detect an English accent?" I asked our host.

"Indeed. I am the proverbial pasty Pom longing for warmer shores. Where are you from, my dear lady?" he asked and kissed my hand.

"California."

"Ah, another sunshine state I adore."

"How long have you lived here in Cancun?"

"I'd say about ten years, now. I just adore the lifestyle."

"You have a beautiful home."

"She's not here for you, Adam," Mateo grinned and rested his hand on the small of my back.

The heat from his palm sent a shiver down my spine and answered the question I'd had about the chemistry between us.

"Oh, you greedy bugger," Adam laughed.

"Come on, Peyton. There's something I'd like to show you."

"Have fun you two," Adam grinned and continued to laugh from his gut.

"He's quite a character," I said once we were out of earshot.

"A very rich man. And an incurable flirt," Mateo added.

"Are you jealous?"

"Should I be?"

"What did you want to show me?" I asked, changing the subject.

Mateo smiled and took my hand. He led me outside to a sprawling lawn and walked toward a viewing deck.

"Cancun as you've never seen her before," he cooed proudly.

I had to give him points. The view was something else.

"Wow."

"I want to kiss you, beautiful Peyton."

My heart skipped a beat and my knees buckled a tad when Mateo pulled me closer. He placed one hand just above my backside and touched my cheek lightly with the other. I assumed he was waiting for an answer.

I didn't say a word, rather moved in and touched my lips gently to his. That was all the consent the sexy Mexican needed. He kissed me passionately while I struggled to keep my legs from failing.

Damn that accent!

* * *

The next few days were a blur. Mateo quickly became a fixture in my Mexican experience. He showed me *his* Mexico, as he called it, and I had to admit that there was a definite advantage to having my own, gorgeous tour guide.

Alyssa didn't complain too much, as Gabriel turned out to be the perfect mixture of fun and bangability in one handsome package.

Days were filled with exploring the locale, sampling the delicious cuisine, and frolicking at the beach, followed by nights filled with dancing and rip-roaring orgasms.

"I tell you, Peyton, this is the life. I wish we could stay here forever," Alyssa sighed one morning when she and I had popped out to the market for eggs and tortillas.

"I know what you mean. I love it here."

"I'm sure Mateo would be happy if you stayed," she winked. "The two of you seemed to be joined at the hip."

"He's amazing, Alyssa," I gushed.

"You're glowing. Do you know that?" she laughed.

"What can I say? Multiple orgasms clearly agree with me."

"You shameless hussy!"

"Oh, please. Don't tell me you and Gabriel aren't going at it hammer and tongs, Miss Priss. I can hear you, you know. The walls are thin."

Alyssa laughed from her gut.

"Oh, my! The man is a raging bull in the sack. I can't get enough of his Mexican burrito. I wish I could bottle him and take him home. I'm sure going to miss his fabulous instrument. Is it me, or am I limping?"

"You are a bad girl, Alyssa Collins," I laughed.

"You better believe it."

"I think I may stay on for another week or two. Mateo wants to take me to Mexico City where he lives."

"Careful, now. Before you know it, you'll be barefoot and pregnant, preparing Mateo's Huevo Rancheros every morning until you're old and gray."

"Would that really be such a bad thing?"

Alyssa stopped walking.

"Are you crazy? You've wanted to be a doctor since you were able to spell *scalpel*. Are you telling me you're ready to give up that dream for a man you've known for a week?"

"Oh, don't be melodramatic. I didn't say I was going to give up my dream for Mateo. Besides, if we do end up together I can always be a doctor in sunny Mexico. There are hospitals here, you know."

"True. All I'm saying is slow down. How much do you know about this guy? He could be married. Have you checked his ring finger for a tan line?"

I laughed at my goofy friend.

"Seriously! All I'm saying is be careful, Peyton."

"Of course, I'll be careful. Now hand me that tomato over there. The one that looks like it has two buttcheeks."

* * *

"You are exquisite, my American beauty," Mateo breathed hard as soon as he got his breath back.

"You're not half bad yourself," I said, equally out of breath.

The man was intelligent, articulate, romantic, and thoughtful, and the sex was mind-blowing. Something told me I'd struggle to find another gem like Mateo Garcia.

It had been a month since we met at the club and honestly, I couldn't imagine my life without him. I had a feeling he felt the same because every time I mentioned that I'd have to get back to the States and start my residency, he'd beg me to stay a little longer. And I would.

Mateo's house was spectacular. I had no idea when we first met that he was so wealthy. I was wined and dined and wooed, and damn it, I liked it.

"I'm taking you to my favorite wine farm this weekend," he purred and kissed my naked stomach.

"I have to go home, Mateo."

"After the weekend. Okay?"

"Okay."

We were walking through the vineyard when he dropped to one knee and presented me with a rock of a diamond.

"Marry me, Peyton," he said with a smile.

"Oh, Mateo! It's stunning," I said as I stared at the engagement ring.

"All you have to do is say yes, and it's yours."

"Yes."

My lover lifted me off my feet and cradled me in his arms."

"I'm going to make you the happiest woman in the whole of Mexico," he said and kissed me passionately.

I'd never been that happy in my entire life. I couldn't believe it. Peyton Garcia. Who would have guessed it?

2

PEYTON

"I'm struggling to believe that you're doing this," Alyssa said while she slid pins into my hair to secure the veil. "Are you sure, Pey?"

"I'm sure, Lyssa."

I am, aren't I? Are you kidding? Yes? You're sure.

"It's not too late to make a run for it," my mother joked and straightened the train on my dress.

"Mom, please. I'm nervous enough. Ugh! I hope I don't trip over this hem and fall off the landing into the ocean. I told the dressmaker to shorten it. I really have to work on my Spanish."

It was my wedding day, and we were in picturesque Puerto Vallarta. My handsome groom was with his best man and my dad who was waiting for me to make my appearance. Mateo and I had decided to have an outdoor wedding under the perfect, blue Mexican sky.

My handsome man had gone all out and I couldn't think of a single thing he'd missed to make this the perfect day for his deliriously happy bride. The flowers, the food, all perfect, including my husband-to-be.

Mom wiped away a tear as she stood back and took the majesty of my dress.

"You are the most beautiful bride I've ever seen, my angel girl."

"Ah, no, Ma! Come on," I said softly and hugged her. "Don't cry. You know my plumbing is suspect. If you cry, I'm going to lose it too."

"I can't help it, darling. You know I'm a bubbler at the best of times."

"Snap out of it, you two," Alyssa said sternly. "You're not going to ruin your makeup, Peyton. Besides, what will Mateo think when he lifts your veil, and your eyes look like two pissholes in the snow?"

I burst out laughing. Alyssa had that effect on me. No matter what the situation, she could always drag a giggle out of me. Thank God for good old Alyssa.

"Okay, let's get this show on the road," I said and straightened my form, hoping it would add just enough height to my stature so that I wouldn't step on the hem and go ass over kettle down the aisle.

"I'll tell Dad you're ready," Mom said and left the room.

"This is it, babes. Soon you'll be Peyton Garcia. Man, what a trip."

"It's surreal, isn't it? I keep pinching myself."

"Promise me something, Peyton."

"What?"

"Promise me you'll let me know how you're getting on."

"Why do you say that, Alyssa?"

"No reason. It's just…well, you're going to be so far away from me. I guess I'm gonna miss you, is all."

"Aah, Lyssa. I'm going to visit often. I promise," I said and hugged my friend as tightly as I could.

"You'd better!"

There was a soft knock on the door.

"Honey, are you ready?"

It was Dad.

"Yes, Dad. I'll be right out."

I took one last look in the mirror and bade a final farewell to Miss Taylor. Onwards and upwards!

"Oh, my goodness, my princess. You look stunning."

"Thank you, Dad. How's Mateo holding up?"

"So cool and calm, you'd think he's done this before. How are you feeling?"

"A little nervous."

"Just a little? I was a wreck on my wedding day. Needed a few shots of whiskey to settle the old nerves. I got a hairy eyeball from the minister. He must have smelled the Irish courage on my breath," Dad chuckled.

"It's a shame Mateo's parents can't be here today. They would have loved you."

"That's so sweet of you to think about that, Dad."

Mateo's parents died when he was a teenager. I imagined they would have been incredibly proud of the fine man their son turned out to be.

"Is it hard, Dad?" I asked.

"What? Marriage? Nahhh. Nothing's hard when you find your soulmate, sweetheart."

Was Mateo my soulmate? I must have thought so. I certainly wouldn't leave my country, my family, and my friends behind if I hadn't believed as much.

"Ready, my love?"

"Ready, Dad."

* * *

I woke up and looked at the nightstand. What? No coffee? You agree to marry them and then they start slipping, I thought. Perhaps I was spoiled. Mateo had left a cup of coffee for me on my nightstand every morning since the first one we'd woken up to together. It was so sweet of him.

I turned to his side of the bed, hoping to find him there, his soft, wavy hair all over the place. But his side was empty. We were back home in Mexico City after a fantastic wedding and honeymoon. I was sad to see my family off and I did have a little cry when Alyssa left too, but that was life.

After a long, lazy stretch, I got out of bed and went for my morning tinkle. I looked for Mateo's usual good morning love note when I went downstairs, but there was none. He must have had a crazy day planned and forgotten to leave me one.

The ladies from the cleaning service, who came three times a week, were busy with their usual tasks.

"Good morning, Mrs. Garcia," one of them greeted me with a nervous smile.

"Hello," I smiled and made my way to the coffee machine.

I was starving, so I rummaged through the fridge for breakfast. Now that I was the woman of the home, I supposed I'd have to make sure that there was food at the ready. My mom had always been in charge of our family's meals. We were spoiled for choice as kids. I remembered the warm feeling I'd get as soon as I stepped through the front door after school to the smell of her cooking. I wanted my family to have that.

Coffee in hand, I went outside to the patio and called Mateo's phone.

"Yeah," he answered, rather harshly.

"Sorry, babe. Is this a bad time? Are you busy?"

"Can't talk now," he said and ended the call.

Wow! That was rude. I made a mental note to give him lip when he got home from work. That was no way to talk to me. I was already having words with him in my head when I heard the sound of something shattering inside the house.

I leaped up and charged to the living room. One of the maids was in a tizz, picking up pieces of a shattered vase and rambling on incessantly in Spanish.

"I so sorry," she kept saying.

"It's alright. I'm sure it was an accident," I told her.

Hmm, not the best start to my day, but I was happily married. That was the most important thing. Everything else was gravy.

* * *

Fuck! I was right in the middle of screwing my secretary on the desk when Peyton called. The timing couldn't have been worse. I got rid of my wife and finished the job at hand. I hoped Peyton wasn't going to be one of those clingy wives who couldn't entertain herself. I mean, what more did she need?

It had been the perfect courtship, a fantastic wedding, and a week of non-stop fucking on our honeymoon. Didn't I deserve a break?

I zipped up my pants and sent my secretary on her way. She was a sexy little thing with big tits and doe eyes who was willing to do anything I asked of her. I liked that in an assistant. I made sure she was always keen by buying her a few shiny trinkets here and there. As far as I was concerned, we had the perfect arrangement.

I called Peyton back an hour later. I wasn't in the mood for drama when I got home, so I thought I'd schmooze her a little to save myself the headache later on.

"Hey, babe. I'm sorry I snapped at you. I don't know what I was thinking. Can you forgive me?" I said when she answered the call.

"Okay, I'll forgive you. Just this once," she said, and I could hear from her voice that she was smiling.

"How about I make it up to you tonight?"

"I like the sound of that."

"Dinner out?"

"Fabulous."

"I'll see you later, darling. Love you."

"Love you back."

Okay, with that out of the way, I got on with my day. My job demanded a lot. I had mountains of pressure on me to keep my wits about me. Not that I couldn't handle it, mind you. I enjoyed having a few balls in the air all at once. I loved the rush of adrenaline required to keep them all up there.

I left the office at 4 pm. If I was going to be the best husband I could be, I'd have to stop off for a quick pick-me-up before I went home. I drove to the old square downtown where I could scratch that old itch without any fear of judgment or retribution.

I parked and walked into Club Hermosas Damas.

Hmph! Beautiful ladies.

Most of them were, I guess. Some were just gals doing their best to nip and tuck enough to keep the fellas coming back for more pussy. Sure, I was there for that, but truth be told, I was after a bit extra. And it was that extra bit that cost me a small fortune.

"Ah, bienvenido, Señor Garcia! We haven't seen you in a while."

"Is Cindy available?" I asked, forgoing the irritating pleasantries.

"Si. Of course. Come in, please. I'll get her ready for you," the rotund man behind the desk said as he gestured for me to take a seat in the private lounge.

"I'm in a hurry."

The man nodded and scurried away down a passage. He was back five minutes later with a knowing grin plastered across his fat face.

"Come, please. Cindy is ready for you."

He led me to my usual suite where he stood back and waited. I took out the precise amount of cash from my pocket and placed it into his grubby paw.

"Gracias," he grinned and left the room.

The suite was the finest money could buy. My money. I heard the door open behind me and turned.

"Hello, handsome," a beautiful redheaded woman with a broken English accent purred as she entered.

"Hello, Candy," I smiled, hard as a rock at the thought of what was to come.

"I've missed you," she cooed.

"Yeah, I've been a little busy."

"Too busy for Cindy?" she pouted and moved seductively closer.

Cindy knew exactly what I wanted. We had a routine. She dropped to her knees and unzipped my pants. She took out my cock and sucked it, then stopped. She stood to her feet, paused for effect, and then slapped me hard across the face.

The burning sensation on my cheek was akin to the best cocaine I had ever had. I grabbed her by her wrists and threw her across the room. The whore landed with a thump.

"You slut!" I shouted at the cowering woman on the ground.

I took off my shirt and pants with urgency and made my way to where she lay.

"Come here," I barked and grabbed her by the hair.

Cindy squealed as I yanked her up and threw her against the wall. I ripped her gossamer gown off her body and slapped her hard on her peachy ass. She let out a soft cry as the slap left a red welt on her butt cheek.

"You've been a bad bitch, haven't you?"

"I'm sorry, baby," she cried as I picked her up and shoved my cock into her mouth.

"Make it better," I groaned as she pleasured me.

She stopped suddenly and pulled away. I grabbed her and threw her onto the bed, face down. I was so hard I could have used my dick as a jack to lift a car.

The whore tried to break free from my grip but I held her down and bit the back of her shoulder so hard I drew blood. She screamed from the pain while I rammed her until I came with a roar of pleasure.

She lay on the covers while I dressed. Her shoulder was bleeding where I'd bitten and her cheek was swollen where I'd hit her.

"I'm sorry if I was a little rougher than usual, baby," I said.

I didn't want to ruin a good thing so I threw a few bills down on the nightstand. She smiled and took it.

"Thank you, handsome," she managed.

I had a shower and got dressed while she lay there. I was ready to go home to my wife.

3

PEYTON

I didn't see the punch coming. It took me completely by surprise. The momentum threw me to the floor where I lay on the expensive living room Persian rug, worried that the blood streaming from my nose would ruin its intricately hand-woven perfection.

Can you believe it? I was more worried about the fucking rug than I was about the fact that my husband had just assaulted me. And why? Because it was somehow my fault that the cleaning staff broke his precious vase. According to Mateo, I should have kept an eye on them, as opposed to lying around all day doing nothing.

What the fuck!

My husband stormed off while I lay there… bleeding and speechless. It took me a while to get up. What had just happened? How did we go from, "Hi, babe. How was your day," to my soulmate throwing a punch in my direction? Who was this man?

I heard the front door slam and assumed it was safe to get up and go to my bathroom to assess the damage the brute had done to my face. I thought about the interview I had with the head of the resident department at the local hospital in two days. How was I going to explain this?

I hardly recognized my reflection in the vanity mirror above the bathroom sink. I fell back instantly on my medical training and checked if my septum was broken. Thank God it wasn't, although I knew I was going to be sporting a shiner where the blood vessels under the skin had shattered.

"Ouch! Son of a bitch!" I yelped as I touched the tender area.

I made a decision right there and then to cut my losses and get as far away from Mateo Garcia as possible. I cleaned my face, took a few Ibuprofens for the pain and swelling, and threw some clothes into a bag. That was the easy part. The hard bit would come later when I'd have to make a decision about my disastrous marriage.

Twenty minutes later I grabbed my car keys and headed for the front door. That's when the depth of the shit I was in sunk in. Mateo had locked me in. To say that the security system at our home was advanced, was an understatement. The place was locked up tighter than a miser's asshole.

I tried several exit routes but to no avail. I was worse off than Rapunzel, and there was no knight in shining armor to save my sorry, beaten ass.

Worst of all, I couldn't even call the cops and report the maniac. Mateo and the commissioner were tight, so tight in fact that the latter was a VIP guest at our wedding. I knew instinctively whose side Pedro would be on.

I didn't want to call my parents or Alyssa because I would never live down the humiliation of admitting that I'd made a terrible mistake by marrying a man I barely knew. Could I have been a bigger idiot?

All that was left was for me to take myself off to the spare room and suck it up. I'd have to wait until Mateo came to his senses and then make a move. When the shock of what had just happened wore off, I started crying. Not out of self-pity, but out of pure anger.

I wasn't sure at what point or hour I fell asleep but when I opened my eyes, it was morning and Mateo was nowhere to be found. I got up and went to the bathroom. Yup. There it was. A shiner of note. I looked like I'd had my butt whooped in a boxing ring.

Mateo was MIA that whole day and, frankly, I wasn't too upset about it. Okay, that wasn't entirely true. I was half expecting a truckload of roses to arrive with a gold leaf-bordered card attached that read,

>*'Please, I beg you for forgiveness, Peyton,'*

or at the very least,

>*'My love, I have no excuse. I'll explain later',*

or some such thing. But, there was nothing—nothing but silence and a locked house. I made spaghetti with butter and black pepper for dinner and went to sleep.

I woke up the next morning to the sound of Mateo's voice coming from downstairs. He was talking to someone on his phone. His tone was as normal as it used to be when he and I had first met. It was unnerving, to say the least.

What was I to do? Stay there and pretend I was asleep? Get up and confront him about not only hitting me but also locking me inside our home for two nights and a full day? I heard footsteps coming up the stairs. My whole body went rigid. I'd never been fearful of anyone before, but this was new territory for me.

"Good morning, my love. We're joining Pedro and his wife for dinner at 8 pm. I have to work late so I'll fetch you just before then," he said, cool as a cucumber, and went to the bathroom.

What! Was he nuts? Great. I married a fucking psychopath!

I didn't know what to say—so I said nothing. When he was done in the bathroom, he walked across to me, kissed me on the cheek, and then went to his closet. Once he'd changed into fresh clothes, he turned and faced me again.

"It's okay. I've let it go. But, please, be more attentive the next time the cleaners are here. What time are you going to the hospital?"

I had to suppress a hysterical outburst. A screaming shit fit was bubbling far too close to the surface for comfort. Was he mad?

He started walking toward me again, and I must have flinched when he raised his hand to move a strand of my hair out of my face because he looked genuinely surprised.

"What's wrong?" he asked me.

"Are you fucking joking?"

"What do you mean?"

"Mateo, you punched me! Look at my face. How can you act as if nothing happened?"

"I'm sorry about that, Peyton. I lost my cool. It won't happen again."

"You're sorry? Really? Is that all you're going to say?"

"I mean it, Peyton. I'm truly sorry."

It suddenly became clear to me that I was attempting to flog a dead horse.

He looked at me with a strange expression.

"I know what you're thinking, Peyton, and I must warn you that it's in your best interest to stay. I will not allow you to leave me. Ever. I love you too much."

My husband smiled and then left the room without pomp and ceremony, leaving me agog and shaky. I knew what he was hinting at. His veiled threat hadn't fallen on deaf ears.

You've made up your Egyptian cotton bed sheets, Peyton.

* * *

My interview with the head of the medical residency at the hospital went well. He offered me the position and I took it. I figured the less time I spent around Mateo, the better. It would give me time to consider my options.

I made a friend too, which was much needed as I was a stranger in a foreign land—and not just literally speaking. Lula was a fellow doctor doing her residency too. She was a year ahead of me, but we got along well and spent a lot of time together at the hospital.

She was a sweet, bright woman, born in Todos Santos, a small village in Mexico with a population of roughly six-and-a-half-thousand people. Her small stature belied her feisty nature.

We were getting dressed into our scrubs one morning as we were about to join a surgeon in the theater. I was always careful to hide my bruises, but I must have been careless that morning.

"What the hell are those?" Lula asked and pointed to my ribcage.

"Oh," I said and covered my torso as quickly as I could. "I bumped myself on the fridge when we were moving it," I lied.

"Mierda! Try again."

"It's not bullshit. I'm telling you. I can be a clumsy dunce."

"Peyton, in the six months I've known you and worked alongside you, you have never once acted like a clumsy dunce. It's your husband, isn't it?"

This was my chance. My one and only chance to share my grief and pain with someone. The question was, was I brave enough?

"You can talk to me, Peyton. Whatever you tell me stays between us."

"He's clever, Lula. He never hits me in places where it will show," I sighed and sank onto the bench in front of the locker. "You know, I never imagined I'd be one of those women who'd allow a man to abuse me."

"No woman ever imagines that, Peyton. Abuse is a process—it's gradual. The bastards start slowly and before you know it, you're forgiving all sorts of things in the name of love and saving face."

"Sounds like you know a thing or two about it."

"Oh, yes. Too much."

"What did you do, Lula?"

"I got the hell out of there and moved as far away as I could."

"I wish I could do that."

"What's stopping you? Apart from you, of course."

"I'm pregnant."

"Fuck. That does change things a tad."

"I know, right."

"What are you going to do?"

"I have to tell him. Perhaps he'll be less of an asshole if he knows I'm carrying our baby."

"I hope so. For your sake and the baby's. But, Peyton," Lula said and held my hand, "I wouldn't bank on it if I were you. I'm sorry, you may not want to hear this, but you can coat a turd in powdered sugar, but it will always be a turd."

"Yeah, I figured."

"Promise me you'll call me if you need help."

"Thank you, Lula. I promise."

It was sweet of her to offer, but I wasn't going to unleash Mateo's fury on anyone else. Besides, I'd learned how to handle my volatile husband. Things were honestly getting better.

* * *

Mateo and I had just made love. I couldn't believe that he could be that tender. It was as if the old Mateo was back. Had we finally settled into some kind of normalcy? I was more hopeful than ever.

"I have a surprise for you, babe," I said.

"I don't think anything can top the surprise you just gave me, but okay. I'm all ears."

I opened my nightstand drawer and took out the third pregnancy test I'd done that morning. The line was dark and unmistakable. I handed it to him with a great deal of pride and enthusiasm.

Mateo stared at the stick for a while and then back at my smiling face. The look in his eyes scared the crap out of me.

"What the fuck is this?" he growled.

I was so stunned by his reaction; I couldn't speak for a moment.

"You're pregnant? What the fuck would you go and do that for? Our lives are perfect. Why would you go and fuck it up?" he shouted.

"I…"

Mateo snapped the test in half and threw the pieces at me. Then, he leaped out of bed, got dressed, and disappeared into the night, leaving me utterly shell-shocked.

Count your blessings, you fool. At least he didn't beat the crap out of you this time!

4

MATEO

"**S**tupid cunt!" I shouted as I gripped and wrung my steering wheel so tightly my knuckles went white.

How was this possible? Peyton was on the pill. Did she lie to me about that? I saw her take the fucking things every morning.

The last thing I wanted was a bloody kid. No little snot-nosed brat was going to ruin my fucking lifestyle. I had enough experience at the orphanage with fucking brats. Kids everywhere were the same—worthless noise bags! It was a deal breaker for sure. I wasn't going to flush my hard-earned money down the toilet providing for kids. I was stuck in a nightmare. This whole marriage thing was a mindfuck.

Peyton was an intelligent woman. A doctor, no less. I was sure she was committed to her profession—that's why I married her. Now, she was ruining everything. A fucking baby! There was only one way forward. Peyton would have to get rid of the kid.

Fuck! I was so stressed. I called Pedro.

"Hey, buddy," he said when he answered.

"I need a fucking drink. You up for it?"

"Of course."

"Meet me at the club."

Pedro and I got each other. He wasn't a pussy like Gabriel. Pedro was a man's man, like me. We knew how to keep our women in line.

I met Pedro in a private room at the club. We gambled there often without any hassles. My friend's position in the police force did come in handy—no one fucked with us.

"What a night," I said and sat down at the poker table.

"What's wrong, mi amigo?"

"Fucking women. They're all the same. Put a ring on their finger and they turn into fucking incubators."

"I'm sorry to hear of your troubles, Mateo."

"Yeah, me too. Anyway, let's play."

The dealer, a pretty blonde with small tits, shuffled the cards and dealt Pedro and me each a hand. I was feeling better already. I would deal with my marital problems later.

After we gambled until 2 am, Pedro and I paid a visit to our favorite spot, Club Hermosas Damas, where Cindy and her entourage entertained us, the way that real women were meant to do for their men.

I went straight from there to my office where I had a shower and changed my clothes. I spent the day at my desk, making money. It was 4 pm when I called it a day and drove home. Peyton wasn't there. I imagined she was keeping herself busy at the hospital.

It was hot out, so I had a swim. Afterward, I poured myself a drink and flicked through the sport's channels. I'd worked up a decent hunger by the time Peyton arrived at 6 pm.

"What's for dinner?" I asked as she set her bag down.

"I'm not hungry."

Was she looking for a fight?

"I didn't ask if you were hungry. I asked what's for dinner."

"I'm not feeling great, Mateo. Would you mind ordering in?"

"You'd feel a whole lot better if you got rid of that parasite you're carrying."

"I'm going to bed," she said and walked toward the stairs.

"I'm seeing the gynecologist tomorrow for my first scan. Please, come with me, Mateo."

"I'm busy."

"Please, babe," she said again, but I turned up the volume on the TV to drown out her whining.

I had a good mind to drag her by the hair and drown her in the pool. It was lucky for her I'd had too much to drink on an empty stomach.

* * *

"Good morning. I'm Peyton Garcia, here to see Dr. Mendes."

The reception area was full of expectant couples. Happy faces and hands resting across swollen abdomens. I forced down the growing lump in my throat as I watched one husband kissing his wife's cheek tenderly.

"Yes, please, take a seat, Mrs. Garcia, and fill out this form."

"Dr. Garcia," I mumbled.

The receptionist gave me an apologetic smile. She was right to ignore my credentials. After all, what kind of professional was I when I allowed my husband to use me as a punching bag? I didn't deserve the recognition or the respect. A swift kick in the pants would have been a more fitting course of action.

I completed the questionnaire and handed the papers back to her. Then, I sat down and waited for my turn. The doctor was running behind, which gave me more time than I needed to contemplate my dire situation.

I thought about the conversation I'd had with Alyssa when I discovered that I was pregnant. Nothing was ever real until I shared it with her. My older sister, Madison, and I were never really close as sisters. We were very different people. Not that we didn't get along, but somehow, I found myself sharing more intimate things with Alyssa.

Besides, Madison had two children already and sometimes, when I was feeling particularly sensitive, it seemed like my older sister lorded that over me. I was probably being ridiculous, but who knew the psyche behind sibling relationships? Especially those of the same gender.

Alyssa was thrilled about the news. She loved kids and planned on having dozens of them once she'd found Mr. Right. I, on the other hand, had always hoped to be at least a few years into my own practice before having a kid. The baby inside me had been a complete fluke. Not planned at all. In fact, I was shocked when I found out I was pregnant.

I'd been on the pill since I left high school. I guess I was one of the nine percentiles of women whose bodies didn't care to follow the rules as set out for them by science.

"Mateo must be so excited," Alyssa gushed.

"Uh, yeah. He is," I had lied, glad that my best friend couldn't see my eyes.

Next, I called my parents. They were over the moon with joy. I pretty much lied through my teeth to them too. It seemed that I was becoming a consummate liar.

"Dr. Garcia. Dr. Mendes is ready to see you now."

I looked up to find a nurse standing in front of me. She led me to a room where she took my blood pressure and asked me if I'd be able to give them a urine sample. That was no problem at all.

I sat down at the desk after that and waited for the doctor to see me. A Beautiful woman with jet-black hair and dark eyes entered the room.

"Hello, Dr. Garcia," she greeted me with a friendly smile, "I'm Dr. Mendes."

"Good to meet you, Doctor."

"You're American," she said with a smile.

"Yes. I married a local," I answered.

"And how do you like our beautiful city?"

"It's lovely," I said.

Your men, however, are a different kettle of fish.

"I'm doing my residency at the local hospital."

"They have a wonderful team of doctors. I did my residency there too," she said, and I could tell from her expression that she had fond memories. "So, you're having a baby. That's exciting. How far along are you?"

"I think I'm about ten weeks along. I had what I thought was a very light cycle last month, but I guess that was a bit of spotting."

"Okay, let's have a look. Would you lie down on the bed for me please?"

I did as she asked. She squirted cold lube on my lower abdomen and moved the ultrasound's transducer over it until she found what she was looking for on the monitor.

"Hello, little one," she said and smiled at me. "There's your little flatfoot."

I opened my eyes and I looked at the monitor with a mixture of joy and trepidation. My baby—Mateo's and mine.

"How far along am I?"

"You were right. Looks to be about three months."

"Is the baby normal?"

I wasn't sure why I used that word, 'normal.' It was an innocent little soul. Even if its daddy was a psychopath.

"Perfectly. Everything is exactly as it should be. Would you like a picture?"

"That would be nice, thank you."

The printer sprang to life and soon I held an image of my baby in my hands. It was a surreal moment. What should have been one of the happiest days of my life was marred by pain and sadness. A baby deserved two parents who loved and wanted it.

Mateo wanted me to abort our child. I'd fought him every step of the way. There was no way in hell I'd kill my child because he was a selfish asshole.

"Dr. Garcia…"

"Sorry…what?"

"Are you alright? I don't mean to pry, but you seem upset."

"It hasn't been the best of weeks. I'll be okay. Thank you for asking."

"Pregnancy is a wild ride. I see you are wearing a wedding ring. Was your husband unable to come today? Seeing one's child for the first time is such a wonderful bonding opportunity for new parents."

"I'm afraid Mateo couldn't make it."

"Mateo?"

"Yes. Mateo Garcia. That's my husband's name. Why? Do you know him?"

I certainly wasn't an expert in reading people, but there was definitely a shift in Dr. Mendes' attitude when I mentioned Mateo's name.

"What's the matter?" I asked.

"Is your husband an investment banker?"

"Yes. Why?"

Okay, I was starting to freak out just a little.

"This is none of my business, Dr. Garcia but I feel I should mention something to you. Seeing as you're not a local and probably haven't heard the rumors."

"Rumors? What rumors?"

"Did your husband tell you that he was married before?"

"Married?"

What was she talking about? Surely, he would have mentioned it. I wondered if she wasn't thinking about someone else by the same name. Mateo was a common name after all.

"Yes. Twice, in fact."

"Are you sure?"

"Yes, I'm sure. I remembered the name because I heard it on the news."

"What do you mean?"

"Both of your husband's wives vanished into thin air."

I felt a chill settling in my bones. I began to tremble.

"The thing is, Peyton. May I call you Peyton?"

"Yes, yes, of course."

"The thing is, both of them were foreigners, and pregnant at the time of their disappearance. I know that for a fact because they were patients of mine."

The room started to spin, and it felt like someone was squeezing my head in a vice. I must have looked a terrible sight because the doctor rushed up to me and put my head between my legs. Was I hyperventilating?

I felt her rubbing my back and talking slowly and deliberately to me.

"It's okay, just take a nice deep breath for me. Slowly. That's it."

She waited a while and then gave me a glass of water.

"Here you go, Peyton. Take a few small sips. That's it."

"I...I don't know how this is possible," I said, struggling to get my breathing under control.

"Again, I'm so sorry to be the one to tell you this, but I won't forgive myself if something happens to you and I said nothing."

"What did the newspapers say?"

"Just that the women were reported as missing and no one, including their families, has ever heard from them again."

"Was there some kind of investigation at least?"

"I'm sorry. I don't know much else. I wish I could help you more, but..."

What was supposed to be a happy day had turned quickly into a nightmare. Two wives! Two! Where the hell were they? Were they

33

hiding somewhere? Did Mateo's psychopathic behavior force them to flee with their unborn children?

And what the fuck was I supposed to do now? Go home and pretend that nothing had happened?

"Thank you, Dr. Mendes," I said and got up.

"Please, stay as long as you like. Until you feel better."

"I'll be alright."

No, you won't. You're royally screwed now, Peyton!

5

PEYTON

I was filled with near-debilitating dread when I entered the home that I shared with my husband—the man who was a complete stranger to me. I was supposed to go to the hospital after my appointment with Dr. Mendes, however, that was nearly impossible after what I'd learned.

I called in sick and went home. Actually, I went to a coffee shop first and sat there for hours before I dared to return to the house. I was thankful that Mateo wasn't there.

How ironic. When we were first married, before Mateo had shown me glimpses of his evil nature, I used to get excited when I heard the sound of his car's engine as he approached. But, as time progressed, I grew to fear that sound. Loathe it, even.

I had to know more about my husband's first two wives. Surely, there was something of theirs within the walls of Mateo's house. My first thought was to start in the bedroom. All women regarded their bedroom to be their safe place. A place where they squirreled away everything they held sacred.

Perhaps I'd find something in the corner of a closet or taped to the underside of a drawer. Something! There had to be some trace of the two women that Mateo may have missed.

But, alas, after hours of climbing onto step ladders and peering into the tiny recesses of the darkest and most awkward spaces, I came up empty. Nothing but dust.

Next, I searched the internet for clues. I came across the articles Dr. Mendes mentioned and read through them carefully. Afterward, I'd learned no more than I already knew, which frustrated the hell out of me. How was I going to protect myself if I didn't know what I was up against? I couldn't very well ask Mateo.

I spent the rest of the day on edge. Then, the dreaded sound came my way. Mateo was home. He opened the door and threw down his car keys on the kitchen counter. It was past midnight, and I could tell from the sound of his footsteps that he was plastered. A good time to ask?

"Peyton!" he yelled from the kitchen. "Isn't there anything to eat around here?"

Hello to you too, you asshole.

I pretended to be asleep. I heard the bedroom door open and lay perfectly still. Perhaps he would go away. It was a long shot but what else did I have?

"Hey!" he said loudly and put on the night light. "Get up. I'm hungry."

There would be no peace for me, so I got up and walked past him to get to the kitchen. Mateo grabbed my arm.

"What? No kiss for the man who works so hard for you?" he snickered and planted a wet, alcohol-infused kiss on my lips.

It took a lot of self-restraint not to vomit all over his expensive Italian shoes.

"Hi," I said and pulled away from him. "I'll make you something to eat," I said, hoping that my soothing tone would pacify him.

"That's my girl," he slurred and slapped me on my ass. It stung like a mofo.

He followed me downstairs to the kitchen after he'd relieved himself.

"What did you do today, my love?" he asked me while I was cooking steak and eggs.

The man was crazy. *My love?* Honestly.

I was in two minds about whether I should remind him of the fact that I'd seen Dr. Mendes, and our baby, for the first time. Doing that could result in one of two outcomes. Either he'd continue his good mood, or he'd turn into a monster again and beat the snot out of me. What to do…

I was feeling particularly prickly, so I went for it.

"I saw our baby today," I said defiantly.

Mateo's face told me immediately that I'd flicked the lion's nuts. He looked at me with daggers in his eyes.

"Your baby. Not mine," he hissed.

Fucker! I lost my cool. I'd been trying for a very long time to go with the new flow, but something inside me snapped.

"When were you going to tell me that you were married before, *my love?*" I challenged the drunk man across the counter from me.

Mateo's face was drained of color, but it didn't stay that way for very long. By the time he opened his mouth to spew venom at me, my husband was beet red. I instinctively took a few steps back.

"Who told you that?" he barked.

"Does it matter? Is it true?"

I knew it was, but I wanted to hear Mateo say the words.

"I see you've been a busy little snoop. Yes. It's true. What of it?"

"How could you not tell me, Mateo?"

"Because it's none of your fucking business."

"Are you serious? Who are they? Where are they?"

Mateo leaped across the counter like a madman. I tried to move out of his way, but he was surprisingly quick for a drunk man. He grabbed me by the hair and yanked my head back.

"Let go of me, you bastard!" I yelled at him.

"I've had enough of you, you stupid American bitch!" he snarled at me and slapped me across the face so hard I thought my left eye socket would explode.

I tried to protect my baby by wrapping my arms around my abdomen. Mateo grabbed my wrists and frog marched me toward the garage door. But, instead of going through to the garage door, he headed for a door that had been locked since the day I arrived at our proverbial love nest.

He fumbled with a set of keys in his pocket and pulled out one that fitted the lock. I tried in the meantime to break free from his iron grip, but it was useless. I was a ragdoll in my husband's strong hands.

Once the door was unlocked, Mateo dragged me into an unknown space. He stopped and fumbled for the light switch. Then, as if I were a bag of unwanted goods, he threw me down a flight of stairs. I landed with a thud and blacked out almost as soon as I hit the ground.

* * *

I woke up to an all too familiar smell. When you're a med student, it's the one smell that no one could ever erase from the passages of your mind.

I sat up and looked around, wondering where the foul smell was coming from. I looked up at the top of the staircase landing. I wasn't sure why I did that. It wasn't as if Mateo would have left the door open for me. But, hope springs eternal, as the bard once remarked.

I got up very slowly. My body was bruised and stiff. I had no way of knowing how long I lay there, unconscious and shivering on the cold concrete floor. My watch had a crack in it and it looked like it had stopped when I hit the deck. I was dressed in my PJs and robe, so I didn't have my phone with me either. Shit!

How the hell was I going to get myself out of this mess? Mateo could leave me there to rot and no one would ever know. I must have been in the basement. I'd asked about that locked door when I first arrived at my new home. Mateo told me he'd locked the room as it had mold issues and wasn't safe. I kicked myself now for not having pushed the issue, but what reasons did a new bride have to mistrust her husband?

I fumbled around in the dimly lit space until I found a source of light in the form of a torch. I had to shake it a few times before the batteries connected properly to the copper strip inside the casing of the torch. My lifeline sprang to life so I could use it to try and figure out how I could escape.

The basement was sparsely furnished. A few chairs, an old table, a few boxes, and three large chest freezers.

I opened one of the boxes and found a photo album inside. I pulled up a chair and sat down at the table before opening up and paging through its pages. I recognized Mateo's face right away, even though he had been quite a few years younger when the photos were taken.

Next to him stood a beautiful woman. She looked at him in the same adoring way I had done when he and I tied the knot. I gathered that she must have been the first Mrs. Garcia by virtue of the youthfulness of the bride and groom.

The album was filled with happy photos. I kept looking until I came to blank pages. The album wasn't completely full.

I rummaged through another box and found a second photo album. It was pretty much a repeat of the first one. Happy, happy, then empty.

Who were these women? Where were they now? What had Mateo done to them? I had to know. The basement was my best chance at finding some answers. Did either of the women keep a diary?

The bump on the black of my head was throbbing. I prayed that I could break off a piece of ice from inside one of the freezers and use it to ease the swelling, so I made my way to one of them.

It was when I opened the freezer closest to me that I found the source of the smell I'd detected earlier—it was not the smell of dead rats and other critters as I had hoped. Inside the freezer were the remains of a human being.

I screamed and jumped back. I had seen and handled plenty of cadavers in my four years as a student. That wasn't what scared me. It was the fact that in this case, I knew exactly who the remains belonged to. Mateo's wives!

Oh, God! Help me. I can't do this...

I slammed the freezer door shut and took in a deep breath to try and control the wave of nausea that had me in its vile grip. I didn't have to open the second one to know exactly what was inside. I knew all too well that if I stayed down there in that basement, I would soon join the occupants of the freezers.

Mateo was not only a psychopathic abuser. He was also a cold-blooded murderer.

I had to escape my fate, and I had to do it before my husband awoke from his drunken slumber. I started rummaging frantically through every box and shelf I could reach until I found a screwdriver. Next, I climbed the stairs and unscrewed the door from its hinges. It took longer than I anticipated, but I kept going. My fingers bled and my nails broke but I didn't stop until the door shifted.

The house was silent except for the sound of Mateo's snoring coming from his study. I tiptoed as quietly as possible up the staircase toward the bedroom. I had to grab my purse and change into something more appropriate. I moved lightning-fast through the room, collecting what I'd need for my emergency exit from hell.

I listened carefully before I left the room. Mateo was still snoring. I tiptoed down the stairs and out to the garage through the interleading door from the kitchen. I was afraid that if I used the remote to open the garage door, Mateo would hear me. So, I unhooked the mechanism and opened the door manually. Slowly…

Next, I wedged a shovel under it to prop it up and prayed it would hold while I disengaged the handbrake and rolled my car out of the garage without starting the engine.

Once I had rolled a fair distance from the garage, I started the engine. I was almost free. All that was left was crossing the border into the US.

Please, God. Help me!

6

PEYTON

I was stressed to near breaking point when I saw the long line of cars at the border post. It was close to 5 am and the migrant workers were on their way through to start their day.

I'd been driving non-stop to get from Mexico City to the US border, stopping only to buy water and a snack and trade in my Mercedes for a clapped-out pile of junk. I had no idea if I'd be able to slip through into The US without Mateo's buddies waiting to drag me back to the man who would certainly kill me. I reckoned that if they were looking for me, they would have my car's registration details and my general description.

I watched as I crept ever closer to the front of the queue. I was glad that I'd kept my old passport, showing my maiden name. Hopefully, the guards would be too busy to check my credentials on their system. Besides, Mateo wouldn't imagine that I'd have the balls to leave the country.

It was my turn. I took in a deep breath and steeled my nerves as I drove up to the window. I smiled brightly and made sure my cleavage was showing—a little distraction was a girl's best friend. I handed the guard my passport.

He looked me up and down while I kept my smile as bright as possible. I couldn't blame him for staring more at my face than my cleavage. I wore so much makeup to cover up the new bruises, I probably looked like a porcelain doll. He walked to the back of the car and looked around for a moment. My heart was beating wildly in my throat.

To my amazement, he waved me through. As he did so, the pile of junk I was driving stalled.

Fuck! Fuck! Fuck!

I tried to start it, but all I got was a succession of splutters. I looked at the guard with controlled panic. I tried several times without success. I panicked when another guard started walking toward us.

"Come on, you piece of shit," I mumbled under my breath as I kept turning the key in the ignition.

Please, please, please!

One more turn. And there it was! The engine roared to life and not a moment too soon. I waved an apology and got the hell out of there without burning tracks of rubber into the tar. Once I was safely within the US borders, I got out of the car, kicked a sizable dent in the driver's side door, and destroyed my cell phone and the sim card. Next, I drove to the first store I could find and bought a burner phone to call a cab.

My folks lived near the border, but I couldn't go there as it was the first place Mateo would look for me. It was just after 6 am when I booked into a motel, utterly exhausted.

The room was adequate—a generous assessment—but I was there to crash for a few hours before I made my way to New York. I wanted to put as much distance between me and my psycho husband as possible, and I'd always wanted to see the Big Apple.

I made a tidy profit when I sold my Mercedes, which gave me enough cash to keep me going for a few months. The dealer must have thought I was nuts when I asked him for a cashier's check, but I turned on the charm and told him some bullshit story. I was sure the bruises on my face nudged the odds in my favor.

It was imperative that I found a job as soon as I was settled. Perhaps there was a residency available at one of the many hospitals in New York. I wasn't going to burden my parents with my lot. I should have been more careful in the first place.

Hindsight was a fickle bitch.

I had so much on my mind that it felt as if my world was spinning. So, I lay down on the bed, covered myself with a blanket, and fell asleep. Before I did, I activated the burner phone I'd purchased at the border. After all, I needed a phone to call 911 if Mateo were to burst through the rickety motel bedroom door.

A crashing sound woke me up. I sat bolt upright, and I looked around in a panic, expecting to see someone hovering over me with a gun aimed at my head. Thankfully, I was alone. The noise was coming from the room next to mine. A man's voice was trying to placate that of a scolding woman. She was obviously throwing things at him. Been there.

I looked at my watch. It was just after 8 pm. I'd slept through most of the day, and if given half the chance, I'd easily sleep through another. But there was no time for such luxuries. I had to put a whole lot of gone between Mateo and myself, so I got up and freshened up before I called a cab to take me to the airport.

I bought a flight ticket, cash, to New York, after which I sat down to a meal in an airport coffee shop. I wasn't starving, but I knew I had to put something into my stomach, or I'd become lightheaded.

I wondered while I ate if my baby was okay. Up to that point, I'd forced myself not to give it too much thought. Survival was my main concern. I'd landed really hard on the concrete floor when Mateo threw me down the stairs, but I comforted myself with the knowledge that babies were far more resilient than we gave them credit for.

Instinctively, I ran my hand across my belly. I wasn't far along in my pregnancy, so my stomach was pretty flat, but it was a comforting action, nonetheless.

It's going to be okay, my little angel. Daddy won't hurt us anymore.

My flight was boarding, so I paid the bill and made my way to check in. I decided to call my family once I was safely in New York. It was going to take time to eat humble pie and explain to them that I'd made a colossal error in judgment. Mateo was a master manipulator. I had to give him that. He even had my folks fooled.

I was heartbroken. Not just for myself, but for what might have been. The two women who had fallen for the same coldhearted man, now dead and dismembered in his basement, must have had the same regrets as they realized they were about to die. I felt awful for their families. Surely, the cruelty of killing someone's child was only superseded by keeping their parents from getting closure.

I couldn't imagine what my parents would have done had I suddenly disappeared off the face of the earth. It's the never knowing that eventually kills a father and a mother. Human beings need closure. They need to say goodbye to the dead. I didn't think it was possible to hate Mateo more. I was wrong.

I had five hours of flying time to plan a life without Mateo. Lula was no doubt wondering where I'd gone and why she couldn't get in touch with me. She was the only one in Mexico I would miss. I prayed that Mateo wouldn't hurt her. He was desperate, and desperate men did desperate things.

* * *

JFK airport was teeming with people. It was comforting to hear my mother tongue being spoken. I was getting pretty good at speaking and understanding Spanish, but I knew I wasn't there quite yet. You know you are a native when you start to think in the language you're speaking, and I was still very much an American.

I needed to be careful as I had a ton of cash on me. Would I put it in a bank and wait for Mateo to find me that way? Hell, no! I'd ask Alyssa to open an account for me in her name and use that instead.

I used the web to look for a suitable place to stay in the meanwhile. There was a quaint little apartment advertised, so I called the letting agent and made an appointment to view it. I got lucky as she told me she could meet me there within the hour. I grabbed my modest bag of worldly goods and hailed a cab.

"It's perfect," I told her once I'd made up my mind.

"Wonderful. I need you to fill out a few forms and then it's yours," she smiled.

"How soon can I move in?"

"Right away, I would think. As soon as the paperwork is done."

"Excellent."

I spent the night in a bed and breakfast around the corner from my new apartment. The owner was a sweet old lady who talked my ear off, but I didn't mind.

I called Lula as soon as I was settled.

"Hola," she said in her usual exuberant tone.

"Lula, it's Peyton."

"Gracias a Dios! Peyton! Where are you? I've been worried sick."

"I'm sorry I haven't called you sooner, Lula."

"Are you okay?"

"Yes, I'm fine."

"Where are you?"

"I left him, Lula."

"Thank God for that! What happened?"

"He used me as a punching bag for the last time."

"I'm so proud of you, Peyton. Where are you? Do you need help? Do you need a place to stay?"

"No. I'm okay, thanks, Lula. I don't want to tell you where I am, my friend. It's safer for you if you don't know."

"You're scaring me, Peyton. What's going on?"

"I can't talk to you for too long, but I'm safe, so please don't worry. I'll call you again in a few days. In the meantime, stay away from Mateo. He is a dangerous man."

"Okay."

"Promise me, Lula."

"Sí, sí...I promise. Take care of yourself, my friend."

"You too. Adiós."

"Hasta luego, Peyton."

Now for the difficult phone call. The one I'd been dreading.

"Hello."

"Hi, Mom. It's me."

"Peyton, my love! What a lovely surprise. How are you?"

Fuck, this was going to be tough.

"Mom, is Dad there?"

"Yes. Is anything wrong, darling?"

"Would you put me on speakerphone, please?"

I wasn't going to explain myself twice.

"Sure, darling," she said. I heard the click as she did as I'd asked.

"Hello, my princess. It's Dad. What's wrong?"

"Hi, Dad. I need to tell you guys something, but I want to ask that you let me finish before you ask me any questions. Okay?"

"Alright."

"Sure, my love."

I proceeded to tell my parents what I'd been dealing with since I'd said those two little words that bound me in wedlock to a psychopath. There was a stunned silence once I had finished my tale of woe. My mother was crying—I could tell from the little muffled sobs— although she tried to hide it.

My father was quieter than he'd ever been. I wondered what he was thinking. I made him swear to me that he wouldn't try and confront Mateo. The last thing I needed was for one or both of them to get hurt. I didn't tell them about the bodies I'd found. That was something I knew to keep to myself for the moment.

I was exhausted once I'd hung up. There was just one more thing I needed to do before I took a well-deserved nap.

"Dr. Forbes' rooms. This is Mandy. How may I assist you?"

"Hi. This is Peyton Taylor. I'd like to make an appointment to see Dr. Forbes, please."

"Certainly. Let me see. The doctor is pretty full up."

"I'm sorry, but it's rather urgent. I'm pregnant and I fell."

"Oh, goodness. Okay, I'll squeeze you in at 9 am on Monday morning."

"Thank you, Mandy."

Dr. Forbes was a highly recommended gynecologist. I heard of him when I was at college. Now that I had my appointment set up, I was out like a light the moment my head touched the pillow.

* * *

My head was pounding. What the hell was I doing in my office? The night before was a blur. I looked at my watch—11 am. Fuck! I had to cut down on my drinking. I got up and started toward the kitchen. That's when the events of the night before suddenly came into memory.

So, Peyton had figured it out. I had no idea how, but I should have anticipated it. My wife was a bright one, and, admittedly, a challenge. My first two wives were gorgeous too, but Peyton was smarter than her predecessors. Too smart for her own good. I wondered if she'd found the bodies yet. Perhaps that would shut up her sassy mouth.

It was time to get rid of her. Peyton knew too much. I'd leave her in the basement for a day or two before I shut her up. Permanently.

I opened the fridge to grab some much-needed cold water when something caught my eye.

"What the fuck?"

Something about the door to the cellar seemed off. I moved closer to investigate and that's when I realized that it was open. How the fuck did she...

I ran down the stairs to the cellar only to find it empty. I couldn't believe my bloodshot eyes. The bitch was gone! My wife had somehow managed to jimmy the lock and now she was on the loose. I ran to find my cell phone so I could call Pedro. With a bit of luck, he had her in custody. All wives run to the cops when they're pissy about their marriages.

"Mateo. What can I do for you, my friend?"

"I've got a big fucking problem."

"Oh? How can I help?"

"Peyton's done a runner. Have you seen her down at the station?"

"No. Let me see what I can do. I'll call you back when I have news."

"Thanks, buddy."

Fuck! This wasn't good. Peyton knew the truth, and she could destroy me if she told the wrong people. I had to find her, and fast.

Pedro called me back a few hours later with the news that my wife had somehow passed through the border into America. After shouting and screaming at him about how fucking incompetent his men were, I called a private investigator friend of mine and gave him Peyton's and her parent's details. He promised me he'd find her.

I cleaned up so I could go to the office.

"You've fucked with the wrong man, dearest Peyton. I'm going to make you sorry you ever met me, bitch," I said when I entered the bedroom and saw the wedding band she'd left behind on the dresser.

7

BEN FORBES

"You've got him, Ben!"

Rowan's voice boomed across the room. He was in the first row of seats closest to the arena where I was laser focused on taking down a man who moved like a gazelle. In all my years of competing in martial arts, I'd seldom come across anyone as quick as my current opponent. I watched his eyes closely for that telltale sign all fighters had when they were about to strike.

I waited and watched…waited…and there it was! The spark lasted a mere split second, but I had him. The fight was in the bag. My right heel connected with his chin—goodnight, Nancy. My opponent collapsed to the ground, while I remained standing, pretty damn pleased with myself. After some time he got up and stood on rickety legs. We faced each other and bowed before I left the arena. The victory was sweet.

"Well, you sure whooped his ass good," Rowan chuckled when I joined him in the stands.

"I feel a bit like Ralph Macchio in The Karate Kid," I grinned.

"Sure, if you were twenty years younger."

"Careful, bud or you'll be the next one to taste the business end of my foot."

"You wouldn't do that to a dear friend, would you?" he snorted.

"Absofuckinglutely," I smirked and slapped him on the shoulder blade. "Come on. I need to eat."

I left Rowan for a moment and went to the changing rooms to shower and change out of my karategi. Kicking ass was sweaty work, unlike my day job, which required more brains than brawn. Luckily for me, I got to enjoy both. Being a gynecologist was fascinating work, even if I were the butt of juvenile, lady parts jokes at parties.

The awards ceremony wasn't until much later that day, so Rowan and I left the dojo and drove to a restaurant nearby.

A pretty waitress took our order as soon as we sat down. I ordered steak and vegetables and Rowan a burger and chips. I suspected that my best friend since high school had a tapeworm. The man ate incessantly without gaining an inch.

"You did well today, Ben. Proud of you, buddy."

"Thanks, Ro."

"I bet the guys in your old unit miss your chop suey moves."

"Cute."

"Do you miss army life?"

"Sometimes. You get attached to people when you spend so much time with them. I must say, though, I enjoy private practice more. Specifically, the freedom it gives me to pursue my fighting."

"You've always been a good fighter, Ben. I don't know if your opponents will survive if you have more time on your hands to practice."

I wasn't one to toot my own horn, but I was at the top level of my game. Martial Arts was my passion. All it had taken was one Bruce Lee film when I was a kid, and I was hooked.

"Listen, Bud. I gotta talk to you about something," Rowan announced.

"Sounds serious. What's up?"

"I've been offered a two-year contract in Europe. It's the kind of opportunity that comes around once in a lifetime."

"That's fantastic, Ro."

"Yeah, I'm stoked. But it means we won't see each other much while I'm gone. Are you going to be okay? Or do I have to prepare myself for a deluge of big boy tears?" he smirked.

"I think I'll live, you chop," I laughed. "I'm sure I can hold down the fort for twenty-four months while you're sewing your wild oats amongst the unsuspecting woman folk of Europe."

"Okay, good. So, you're cool."

"Right as rain, you mullet. Besides, Owen will keep me company. I do have a life apart from you, you know."

"In that case, let's arrange a weekend away, just the boys, so we can raise hell before I go. Tell your brother to come along."

"Deal."

* * *

I took a break from training for the rest of the weekend, and spent Sunday bass fishing with my brother, Owen, at St. Lawrence River. Owen and I were as close as brothers could be. He was two years younger than I, so we grew up in each other's pockets. We'd get into scrapes just like other siblings, but the bond we had was special.

"How'd it go yesterday?" Owen asked me while I was casting. "I'm sorry I couldn't be there."

"It was great. Everything okay?"

"Yeah. Suzy's mom had another one of her *episodes*, so…"

"What was it this time?"

"Honestly, I have no idea. That woman is something else."

"You're a saint for putting up with her crap."

"What can I say? Suzy's worth it."

"That she is."

Owen and Suzy had been together for roughly two years. She was an absolute honey, the perfect mate for my brother. But the poor girl had a mother who was madder than a box of frogs. Rich, divorced, spoiled, and an incurable hypochondriac, Suzy's mother made her easygoing daughter's life a nightmare.

"Speaking of women who keep us on our toes, what's happening with your love life?" Owen asked.

"You know I don't have much in the way of free time between work and martial arts training. It seems selfish to get into a long-term relationship. And, even if I wanted to, where would I meet someone?"

"Hello! You have a smorgasbord of women banging down your door every day. You're like the pied piper of pussy, Bro. Are you telling me you haven't met anyone that way?"

"You kiss our mother with that mouth?"

"You bet. Come on, Ben. There has to be someone who's tickled your fancy of late."

"Tell you what. When I meet one who's worth the effort, I'll let you know. Okay?"

"Yeah. You do that."

"Now, shut your pie hole. You're scaring off the fish."

"What? Karate Kid can't catch one with a pair of chopsticks? You're slipping brother."

* * *

Monday got off to a roaring start with a waiting room full of patients. I settled into my office first, then buzzed Mandy to send in the first file.

Hhmm. A doctor. I buzzed Mandy and told her I was ready to consult.

The door opened, and in walked a strikingly beautiful woman with intelligent eyes and a figure that would make most men weak in the knees. Had I met her socially, I would have made a point of introducing myself. But she was my patient now, so no funny business.

"Good morning, Dr. Taylor. I'm Doctor Forbes. Please, have a seat. How can I help you today?"

"Good morning," she said once she was seated. "I'm four months pregnant, but I fell down a flight of stairs, and I wanted you to check on my baby, please."

"When did this happen?"

"Two days ago."

I wondered why she'd waited so long before seeing me. Dr. Taylor answered me as if she anticipated my question.

"I wasn't able to make an appointment right away. I was traveling. I'm new in town."

"I see. Any bleeding or spotting?"

"No."

"Okay, let's have a look. The ultrasound will tell us what we need to know. Please, disrobe behind the screen and make yourself comfortable on the bed."

The beautiful doctor got up and followed my instructions while Patricia, my assistant nurse, entered the room and took her place next to the bed. I gave Dr. Taylor a few minutes to get undressed before I joined the two women.

"Did you have your first ultrasound?"

"Yes. The baby was normal and healthy."

"Good."

I squirted the gel onto my patient's smooth abdomen before I glided the transducer over the area where her uterus was. It didn't take me long to discover that the child inside Dr. Taylor's womb was dead. Damn. I hated this part of my job.

Patricia glanced at me for a second before she turned her gaze back to the monitor. I looked down at Dr. Taylor. She was quiet, but I saw a lone tear trickling down to her ear as she lay on her back, staring at the ceiling.

"Just tell me, Dr. Forbes," she said softly.

"I'm sorry, Dr. Taylor," I said, conveying all the sympathy I allowed myself as a professional, "I can't find a heartbeat. Your baby has passed away."

My being was flooded with an unexpected primal urge to protect this woman. That had never happened to me before. The intensity of it took me by surprise.

Patricia pulled a Kleenex from its holder and handed it to the woman who was doing an excellent job of being brave.

"I'll give you some privacy so you can get dressed," I said, then settled at my desk.

I had to wonder what the circumstances were surrounding her fall. Not that it mattered at this stage. Her baby was dead and now I had to talk to her about the next step. Patricia left the room.

"A DNC?" she asked as soon as she sat down.

"Yes, that would be best. I'm going to book you into the hospital. Mandy will call you with the details."

"Thank you, Dr. Forbes."

"My condolences, Dr. Taylor. You mentioned you were new in town. Do you have anyone here who can support you? I realize that this is a very emotional time. The baby's father perhaps?"

"I'll be fine, thank you."

Something told me the father of the dead child wasn't in the picture. Surely, if he were, he would have accompanied the poor woman sitting across the desk from me to this crucial appointment. This was a big deal. But it wasn't my job to snoop, so I let it go.

"Alright. I'll see you this evening. I think it's best if we do the operation sooner rather than later. Again, my condolences for your loss, Dr. Taylor."

She nodded and wiped away a lone tear from her cheek before she got up and headed for the door.

I watched as she walked away with poise. This was a strong woman. I had no idea what she's been through, but instinct told me it had been a doozy.

I thought about Dr. Taylor throughout the day. I couldn't help myself. She fascinated me. I made arrangements with the theater staff to book a timeslot and prayed that Dr. Taylor was as strong on the inside as she appeared to be on the outside.

8

PEYTON

The floodgates opened as soon as I stepped out of Dr. Forbes' office building. It felt as if someone had plunged a knife into my heart. My baby was dead. I cried for the loss, for the future that might have been, and for all the milestones mothers and their children shared.

It's strange how the mind works. I'd never been envious of Madison's motherhood. But, suddenly, my sister's ability to enjoy her children made me feel like half a woman. It wasn't logical, but I felt it all the same. Bloody hormones.

Come on, Peyton. Pull yourself together. You will have a child someday—with someone worthy of fatherhood. Perhaps this is for the best. You know Mateo would have destroyed your child. No mother should have to live with that kind of fear.

The voice of reason was right. Not that it was much of a comfort to my broken heart at that moment. I returned to my new apartment and spent the afternoon resting and preparing myself mentally for the DNC.

I'd been putting off talking to Alyssa. But it was time. I dialed her number.

"Hey, stranger! Where have you been?" Alyssa asked me when she answered. "Don't tell me you and lover boy were off on another exotic getaway because I'll have to throw up from pure envy."

"Hi, Lyssa. No, I'm afraid not."

"What's wrong? Have you been crying?"

"I don't know where to start. Oh, Lyssa, it's all such a mess."

"What the hell is going on, Peyton? Talk to me."

"I should have listened to you."

"About what? You're scaring me. What are you talking about?"

"Mateo. He's a psychopath, Lyssa. You were right. I should have taken more time to get to know him before I jumped into marriage."

"Tell me what he's done, Peyton."

I didn't quite know where to start. Feeling like an idiot wasn't helpful either. But Alyssa was my best friend and I knew she wouldn't judge me, so I told her everything. Everything except for the bodies in the basement. I wasn't ready to share that yet. I also explained to her why I hadn't gone to the police.

"Oh, God, Peyton! I don't know what to say. I'm so sorry. Where are you now?"

"I'm safe. I'm in New York."

"How can I help you, my friend?"

"I need you to open a bank account for me. I don't want to make it easy for Mateo to track me down."

"Of course. Do you have enough money?"

"Yeah, I'm okay for now. I sold my car. But I'll need to find a job soon. I don't want to burden my parents."

"Don't be ridiculous! I'll help you."

"No, you won't. I have to do this for myself, Alyssa. I made a mistake and I plan on fixing it."

"But, what about the baby? How will you work once you have a newborn to care for?"

"I...I lost the baby."

Alyssa was silent, but I could hear muffled sniffles which set me off again. Together, my best friend and I mourned the loss of my child. It was a while before we spoke again.

"I'm so sorry, Peyton. So sorry. I wish I could kill that bastard."

"You and me both."

"Are you in pain?"

"Not yet. I'm going to have a DNC this evening. I'll call you tomorrow."

"Okay. I love you, my friend. Promise me you'll call me if you need help."

"I promise. I love you too."

I felt a little better after the call. At least someone else knew the truth about Mateo. Alyssa promised to keep it to herself. I didn't want my family to know. Not yet anyway.

Mandy from Dr. Forbes' surgery called me and told me I had to be at the hospital at 4 pm. The procedure was scheduled for 6 pm.

I was nervous, but I knew it had to be done. It was absolutely true that doctors were the worst patients. Probably because we knew all the things that could go wrong during surgery. Ignorance truly was bliss, in this instance. But Dr. Forbes was purported to be one of the best, so I was hopeful.

He wasn't at all what I had expected. For a start, he looked younger than his thirty-eight years. Also, he was insanely good-looking. Tall, dark, in excellent shape, armed with intensely dark eyes, and sporting well a manicured stubble. I guessed the sexy, soft-spoken gynecologist had no shortage of female admirers.

Not that I was on the hunt for a replacement by any stretch of the imagination. Mateo's and my relationship wasn't something I'd planned, as it happened. I should have known better. Who knew? Had I stopped for a moment before leaping, I may have spotted the flaws in my husband's near-perfect facade. I wondered if I'd ever forgive myself.

* * *

"Hello, again," Ben's soothing voice sounded above me as I lay on a gurney in the operating theater.

"Hi."

"How are you feeling?"

"Are you kidding? You know what they say about doctors being patients, don't you?"

"Ben, please. I think as doctors we can forgo the formalities."

"Peyton."

"Okay, Peyton. Are you ready?"

"As ready as I'm ever going to be."

"I've got you," he said and squeezed my hand.

It was unexpected, but at that moment, a slew of feelings coursed through me. It was as if we'd known each other for years. I trusted Dr.

Ben Forbes, effortlessly. What was it about this man that had me so at ease?

A nurse wheeled me into the operating theater, where Ben, the anesthetist, and a team of theater nurses were going through their pre-op rituals.

"Hello, Dr. Taylor. I'm Peter. Are you ready for a wonderful nap?" the anesthetist smiled.

"Don't suppose you have tequila in that IV?"

"Ah, a tequila girl. I'm afraid not, but I do have a lovely little cocktail I think you're going to enjoy almost as much."

"Sounds good. Thanks, Peter."

A nurse set up the drip and placed the needle into a vein in my hand.

"Sorry, it's going to sting a bit," she said.

Sting...yeah, sure. Can't be worse than having the shit kicked out of you by an angry husband.

"Here we go," Peter said. "Countdown from ten for me, please."

"Ten...nine...eight...seven...sss..."

* * *

"Dr. Taylor...can you hear me?"

I tried to open my eyes, but the lids were so heavy. It took me a few attempts. I blinked slowly, trying to focus on the face above mine.

"Ah, there you are. Hello, Doctor. How are you feeling?"

"Jim Dandy," I slurred. "Is it over?"

"Yes. You're in recovery."

I tried to sit up.

"Slowly," the nurse instructed. "The anesthetic will take a while to wear off."

"Where's Ben?"

"Dr. Forbes is in theater. He's busy with another patient. But, he did ask me to tell you that he'll pop in to see you before he leaves."

"Okay. Thanks."

I dozed on and off until they wheeled me through to my ward. There were four beds in the room, with mine closest to the window. All I wanted to do was sleep, but that wasn't the way a hospital operated. Oh, no. Patients were prodded, poked, and woken up at ridiculous hours—all the stuff I had only ever observed and experienced from the other side of the bed.

The nurses had already changed shifts when I arrived in the room. They went about their work while I tried to get some sleep. I was exhausted and felt empty. The tiny clump of cells that was growing inside of me wasn't big enough to miss, but emotionally I felt the void the baby's absence had left.

Someone touched my arm. It was Ben.

"Hi, Peyton. How are you feeling?"

"Like I could sleep for a century. How did the procedure go?"

"It took me longer than I'd anticipated. There was a lot of damage, Peyton."

"What kind of damage?"

"The kind that takes more than one tumble down a flight of stairs to inflict."

I knew what he was asking me, but I wasn't ready to talk about it.

"Please, don't ask."

"Okay," he said and sat down on the edge of the bed.

63

"So, what are your plans, now that you're in New York? Are you going into private practice?"

"I haven't completed my residency yet. I guess I'll have to apply to a few hospitals and see where I can slot in."

"I see. I have a vacancy for a resident doctor if you're interested. Why don't you take a few days to recuperate, and when you're ready, you can call me, and we'll discuss it. Here," he said and pulled a business card from his pocket, "my cell phone number. Call me anytime."

"Thank you, Ben. I'll do that."

"Good. But, for now, I want you to rest. I've prescribed something for the pain. I have to apologize in advance, though. The pharmacy's out of tequila, so I substituted."

"All good, Doc. I can always have some cactus courage when I get home."

Ben laughed, squeezed my hand, and left me in the care of the nursing staff.

This time, when he touched me, I felt a spark. Bloody drugs.

* * *

I called my parents a few days later. They were relieved to hear from me, even though I had to share the bad news about losing the baby with them.

"I'm so sorry, my darling," Mom said.

"Yes. Anything we can do to help, princess?" Dad asked. "Do you need money?"

"I'm okay for now, thank you, Dad. Alyssa opened an account in her name and I'm using it."

"Please, sweetheart, don't be too proud to ask for help."

"I won't be, Dad. Thank you. I'll be back on my feet in no time. As a matter of fact, I've been offered a residency position at the hospital where I had the procedure done. I'm sure I'll be just fine financially once I start."

"That was quick," Mom said.

"I know. I'm looking forward to it. It will be good for me to focus on my career again."

"I agree," Dad said. "In the meantime, send me your bank account details so I can put in a little buffer. Just in case. I'm not taking no for an answer, Peyton."

"Thanks, Dad. I'll pay you back."

"No rush. Be safe, my princess."

A thought suddenly occurred to me.

"Mateo hasn't contacted you, has he?"

"He'd better not if he knows what's good for him!" Dad thundered into the phone.

"Calm down, Frank," Mom cautioned him. "You know your blood pressure will shoot through the roof."

"Don't fuss, Millie. I'm fine."

"Mom's right, Dad. Don't let that monster do any more harm to this family."

We spoke for a while longer before I hung up. It was time to call Ben and accept his job offer. I called his cell number and waited while it rang. I wasn't sure why I was nervous. Must have been because I hadn't worked in a while, and I guessed that all doctors were obsessed with being perfect at their jobs.

"Hello."

"Hi, Ben. It's Peyton."

"Hi, Peyton. I was hoping you'd call."

"I've given your offer some thought, and I accept. If the vacancy is still open, that is."

"Of course. That's great. Come to my office tomorrow morning. I'll ask Mandy to call you to confirm the time. We'll run through the details then."

"Thank you, Ben."

"You're welcome. Oh, how are you feeling?"

"A little tender in the giblets, but I'll be fine."

"You're a strong woman, Dr. Peyton Taylor," he said.

"I don't know about that, but I'm trying."

"I'll see you tomorrow."

"See you."

I felt better after the call. Ben had the uncanny ability to put me at ease.

Alright, Peyton. Here's to getting on with life.

9

BEN

I was shocked when I saw the damage inside Peyton's body. From the old bruises she sported, someone had clearly used the poor woman as a punching bag. I never understood the need a man had to hurt a woman physically, especially someone as beautiful as Peyton. Such perfection deserved to be cherished and celebrated, not abused.

I doubted whether she would ever have children. It would take a herculean surgical effort to correct the scarring her miscarriage would leave behind. I did what I could while I operated on her but there would most certainly be more work to do at a later stage.

I checked my wristwatch. It was half an hour before my meeting with her regarding the residency position. My stomach was in a bit of a knot. What was it about Peyton that made me want to scoop her into my arms and never let her stub even one toe?

Come on, Ben. Get a grip. You are her advisor now. Don't muddy the waters.

I made a few calls to check on my post-operative patients. It must have taken longer than I'd anticipated because a knock at the door told me that Dr. Taylor had arrived for our meeting. I looked up from my paperwork.

"Come in," I called.

"Dr. Taylor is here to see you."

"Thanks, Mandy. Please, show her in."

I'd just closed the files when Peyton walked in, her head high and her back straight. She had such a confident stride. It was hard to imagine anyone bullying her.

"Hi, Peyton. Please, sit down."

"Hello, Ben."

"You look well. I take it you're feeling better."

"Much. Thanks."

"Good, then let's see if we can employ that mind of yours, shall we?"

I discussed the remuneration package with Peyton and gave her a comprehensive rundown of the details of her residency. When we were done, she accompanied me to the hospital where I introduced her to the team she'd be working alongside.

"They seem like a good bunch of people," she said once we were done.

"They're a brilliant team. I'm sure you'll learn a lot from them."

"I intend to."

It was time for me to call it a day.

"I'll see you tomorrow morning," I said once we were done.

"Thank you again, Ben."

"Don't thank me too soon. I'm planning on working you pretty hard, Dr. Taylor," I grinned.

"I look forward to the challenge."

"Can I drop you off somewhere?"

"No thanks. I'll manage."

"Okay. Goodnight."

I left the hospital and drove home. I had an early start the next day, so I caught up on some sleep—a rarity in a doctor's life.

Peyton was at the hospital when I started my rounds early the next morning. She stuck to me like glue while we made rounds, asking questions and making notes. Her face lit up when she was immersed in the details of the patients' diagnoses. It was wonderful to see the passion she clearly had for the subject matter. Peyton was a smart cookie.

I kept an eye on her those first few weeks. She was there when I arrived, and she was still there when I left late after surgery.

"You're allowed to go home every now and again, you know," I said to her when I found her hard at it late one evening.

"I know," she smiled.

"So, how are you finding the job?" I asked, knowing full well what she would say.

"I'm loving it. A little rusty at times, but I suspect that will pass."

"You're doing an excellent job, Peyton. Don't be too hard on yourself or you'll take all the fun out of it for me," I smiled.

"Wouldn't dream of it, Sir," she winked. "Oh," she said when I turned to leave. "Mrs. Riley is showing no signs of consciousness. The poor dear is so old and frail. I hope my family lets me go when I reach her advanced years."

"Yes, the poor woman's son is determined to hang onto his mother for as long as possible."

"I can understand that. I'd hate to lose my mother. But I think that once the quality of life is gone, it's time to stop resuscitating."

"Agreed. Perhaps you can have a gentle talk with Mrs. Riley's son when he visits her next."

"You wouldn't mind?"

"Of course not. I'll be there when you tell him. Patients want to see senior doctors. Human nature, I guess. But I'll leave the talking to you. Are you okay with that?"

"Sure. Thanks, Ben. I'll make an appointment and let you know."

"Great job, Peyton."

I felt good about her appointment. Dr. Taylor had all the makings of an excellent physician. She was only twenty-four, but already other residents and nurses asked her for advice. I could spot a leader a mile off. It was one of the things you learned in the army—spotting a leader.

The more I interacted with Peyton, the more I struggled to get her out of my mind. I had to know who had done her so much harm. But I couldn't very well ask her straight out, so I'd have to come up with a way to get to know her better. I wanted to ask her out to dinner, but that would have been awkward for her.

Once or twice a year, I'd host a barbeque at my house for the resident doctors under me. It was always very well attended, so I decided that that would be my way in with Peyton. The young doctors seemed to relax and let down their hair in social settings. I could only hope that Peyton would follow suit and let me in just a little so I could learn more about her. If she were with her colleagues, she wouldn't feel as if I was crowding her.

I sent out the invitations to the team and all but one replied. I guessed I'd have to wait and see if Peyton changed her mind.

I met Owen for a drink after a training session with Dylon, my martial arts instructor.

"How's your harem?" he chuckled.

"Outstanding, thanks."

"Lucky bastard."

"I tell you, Owen, some days I wish I could use my martial arts moves on the partners of some of the women I treat."

"Why? What happened?"

"Let's just say some men don't deserve to be loved."

"Isn't that the truth?"

"I operated on a patient a few weeks ago. Whatever her man did to her is tantamount to torture. She looked like a punching bag."

"Bastard. What did she say about it?"

"That's the thing. I didn't ask because I could tell she wouldn't have told me anything if I had."

"I find it so strange that women stay with men like that."

"I'm sure they have their reasons. This poor girl lost her baby because of it."

"That's tragic, Ben. I'm sorry to hear that. I could never do your job."

"Mostly, it's rewarding. But, there are times when I can't wait to go home and punch the shit out of something."

"Save it for the tournaments, bud."

After drinks, we had dinner and then I retired for the day. I must have been in the shower when the message came through on my cell phone. It was from Peyton.

Hi, Ben.

Thank you for the invite to the barbeque. What can I bring?

"What the fuck do you mean you haven't found her yet? What am I paying you for, you useless fuck?"

Private dick, my ass! The guy had been pissing about for weeks, looking for Peyton. How hard could it be to find one woman? He knew where her family lived, her best friend, everything! And, still, he had no clue.

I'd managed to trace the Mercedes the bitch sold for a pittance. As for finding my wife, who knew where she was hiding?

"Mr. Garcia, I promised you I'd find your wife, and I will. These things take time."

"I don't have time! You'd better get your head out of your ass and try harder, or they'll be looking for you soon. And, trust me, they won't find you," I snarled and ended the call.

Peyton had simply fallen off the face of the planet. No bank account, no credit card, no DMV address. It was infuriating. Meanwhile, she knew about the dismembered bodies in my basement, and I had no idea who she'd tell. I wasn't worried about the Mexican police. Hell, I had Pedro to cover my ass, but knowing my prickly wife, she'd run to the FBI or something. The last thing I needed was to be hunted by foreign government agencies.

I drained the whiskey glass of its contents and slammed it down on my desk. I was frustrated and in desperate need of some TLC, so I grabbed my coat and headed for the door. Perhaps Club Hermosas Damas could sort me out.

I called Pedro from my car phone.

"Hey, Pedro. Feel like joining me for a game of cards later?"

"Sorry, Mateo. I can't. The fucking police commissioner is here this week, so I have to watch my ass. But you go and have fun. Give the ladies my best."

Oh, well. Lone wolf out on the prowl it is.

Cindy was always happy to see me. The woman could take a beating and still suck a golf ball through a hose. That was my kind of lay. Peyton was so unadventurous when it came to sex. I suggested once that we experiment with a few toys or even throw in another partner, but she put up such a fuss it wasn't worth asking again. Frigid bitch.

"Hey, baby," Cindy purred when she entered the room.

"Come here, bitch," I growled.

The rest of the visit was fantastic—for me anyway. I'm sure Cindy liked it too, or she wouldn't keep coming back for more. That was the thing about whores. They didn't squeal about bullshit.

Fuck knew what Peyton had to complain about. The woman had everything she could ever want or need. I didn't understand her. Perhaps it was time to marry a local. Foreigners were full of shit.

I had to give Cindy a little extra to keep her from crying to her pimp, but it was worth every punch.

My ego was bruised. Peyton had left the tip of her boot in it when she kicked me to the curb. The only way to restore the equilibrium was to find her, beat the snot out of her, and shut her up for good. Until then, I would keep the rage inside of me locked up tightly, away from the world that thought I was the perfect specimen of manhood.

You better enjoy your freedom, Peyton, 'cause I'm coming for you.

10

PEYTON

"Hey, Peyton. Are you joining us at Dr. Forbes' house for a barbeque?"

"Hi, Olivia. Uhm, not sure yet."

"You've gotta come. It's a blast. Last year we all ended up in his pool. It was such fun. He's not one of those creepy types if that's what you're worried about."

I'd received the invitation a few days before. It was pretty much all the residents talked about. I wondered what the fuss was all about. Ben was a nice guy, so I wasn't all that surprised.

Ever since I met him at his office, I couldn't shake the feeling that we had some kind of unusual connection. Perhaps I read more into it than there was. But the way he took care of me and offered me a job spoke volumes about his character.

Uh-huh. You thought Mateo was special too and look where that got you. I would be too quick to fall for another guy, Peyton. Besides, you've got enough on your plate.

"Hello, Peyton."

"Hi, Dave."

"You asked me to let you know when Mrs. Riley's son was here."

"Oh, yeah. Thank you for letting me know."

I wanted to have a chat with Mr. Riley. His mother was so frail, and I knew she was suffering terribly. Her son had power of attorney over her estate and her physical well-being, but clearly, he didn't have the facts. As far as he was concerned, his mother was going to bounce back. She wasn't.

I walked to the room where Mrs. Riley lay, hooked up to countless pipes and monitors. The poor woman looked like a creature out of the series Stranger Things. Her son was sitting at her bedside, talking to someone on his cell phone. I couldn't help overhearing his conversation.

"Yeah, Mom's okay. She's resting. I'm sure she'll be back home soon. Sure, I'll call you tomorrow."

I waited for him to end the call before I cleared my throat. He looked up as if he hadn't noticed me until then.

"Hello, Mr. Riley. I'm Dr. Taylor."

"Hi, Alex Riley," he said and extended his hand.

"May I call you Alex?"

"Of course."

"Thanks. Alex, the head surgeon, and I wanted to chat with you about your mother."

"Why? What's wrong? I don't want to wait for another doctor. Just tell me."

"Alex, I'm sorry to tell you this, but your mother isn't going to get any better. She's frail and her brain activity is all but non-existent. At this stage, her only hope of survival is if she remains on life support."

"What are you saying, Doctor?"

"Alex, I'm saying that it will be better to prepare yourself. Say goodbye to your mom while you can, because as soon as we take her off life support, she will pass. I don't recommend that we resuscitate her again. There's no point. It's time to let her go."

The pain in Alex's eyes filled me with compassion. I moved closer to him and touched his arm.

"It's what's best for her, Alex."

"I can't let her go," he whispered.

"Technically, she's already gone. You don't have to decide right now, but please, think about it. My condolences, Alex."

I left him to process my words and hoped he would come to the same understanding. Alex Riley was the first family member of a patient with whom I'd discussed such a heavy subject. I thought it had gone quite well.

Perhaps it was the feeling of having achieved a significant milestone that spurred me on to accept the invitation to the barbeque. Whatever the cause, I was suddenly looking forward to letting my hair down.

* * *

I rang the doorbell and waited. I could hear the music coming from inside the house. It was probably why no one answered the door, so I opened it slowly and walked in.

"Take whatever you want, just don't hurt us."

"It's a good thing I come in peace," I laughed.

"Hi. Welcome to my home."

"Hi, Ben. Thank you. Where do I put this?" I asked and held up a bottle of tequila.

"You didn't have to bring your own."

"It's not for me. It's a gift."

"How thoughtful. Thank you, Peyton."

"You're welcome. Sounds like the gang's all here."

"Yup. They're out back. Can I offer you a drink?"

"I'd love one."

"What will it be?"

"It's a little early for tequila. I'll have a beer, thanks."

"Sure. Follow me."

Ben's home was beautiful. Hardwood floors, high ceilings, and filled with light. I followed him outside to the pool area where my colleagues were chatting, laughing, and swimming.

"Hey, Peyton," Olivia called from the gazebo. "Glad you could make it."

I waved.

"Did you bring your swimsuit?" Ben asked as he handed me an ice-cold beer.

"I did."

"Good. It will save me from having to dry your clothes when the boys throw you into the drink," he grinned.

"Does it get that rough, then?"

"Not always, but the gang can get a little overexcited."

"It's a good thing there's a doctor on call."

"Funny. How was your day?"

"Good. I spoke to Mrs. Riley's son this morning."

"Okay. How did that go?"

"Better than I expected. He's a nice man. I just don't think he was willing to accept that his mother wasn't going to get well again."

"Let's hope that, now that he has the facts, he'll make the right decision. Well done, Peyton."

"Your home is beautiful."

"Thanks. Would you like a tour?"

"Uh, sure."

"I don't bite. I promise," he smiled.

"Good. I haven't had my rabies shot in a good few years."

"Rabies? Bushbaby childhood?"

"It's a long story."

"Well, I'd love to hear it someday," he laughed.

I followed Ben into the house. I couldn't help noticing his perfect backside. I wondered what he did to keep in such good shape. I found my answer soon enough.

"This is quite a trophy room, Ben," I said when we passed a room filled with medals and photos.

"Oh, yeah. That's where I keep my victor's spoils," he winked.

He said it very matter-of-factly, with no puffed-out chest motions or show-offish gestures.

"Impressive. How long have you competed in martial arts?"

"Since I was a kid."

"You're clearly very good at it."

"I do alright."

"It must be nice."

"What?"

"Having the know-how to kick someone's ass," I said.

"Sounds like that's something you've thought about," he said and straightened one of his photos.

"Haven't we all?"

I looked toward another wall that had several pictures of Ben dressed in a US Military uniform.

"Military?"

"Yeah. I started my career as a military doctor."

"What was that like?"

"I enjoyed it."

"Why did you leave?"

"Being an army doctor is a transient lifestyle. There are only so many times one person can move from one base to another before packing peanuts becomes a drag. I enjoyed it while I was in it, but I missed being close to my family. When my father had a stroke, I realized that I was missing out on too much family life. So, I left and went into private practice."

"The army recruiters came to talk to us when I was in high school. I must say, the idea of working for the army is tempting when you're a kid. My father had a fit when I told him I was considering it."

"It's not an easy life. He probably wanted to protect his daughter. I can appreciate that."

All things considered; I would have been safer in the army than I was with Mateo. At least I would have come away with fewer bruises and a whole heart.

"Come," Ben said, "I want to show you something."

He had the same look in his eyes as a young boy before he showed you his treasured toy collection. I followed him up the stairs, where he stopped in front of a closed door. Then, Ben opened the door and stood aside so I could step into the room.

"This is where I pretend to be Bruce Lee," he said with a naughty chuckle.

It felt as if I'd stepped into a dojo in an old Japanese movie.

"It's where I practice."

"What a beautiful room."

I imagined Ben in his white suit with a black belt around his waist. He must have been quite a fierce opponent to have won all those trophies and medals. Where was he when Mateo was kicking the snot out of me?

"What are those," I asked and pointed to the corner of the room.

"That is an agility ladder. Keeps me on my toes…literally," he smiled. "Then there's a grappling dummy that tends to fight back, a few breaking boards, and a few other bits and bobs."

"Is that a Samurai sword?" I asked and pointed to the wall.

"That is my pride and joy. It's a Samurai Katana I bought when I was in Japan."

"It's stunning."

"Would you like to hold it?"

"I'd love to."

"Okay. But be careful. It's ridiculously sharp."

"You mean, like a scalpel," I grinned.

"Touché."

Ben took the word down from the wall and handed it to me. I was fascinated by the handle.

"The wrap on the handle is called the ito."

"It's so intricate," I said and ran my fingers over the design.

"The sword was made by an old warrior."

"It must have set you back a few paychecks."

"Worth every penny."

I handed the katana back to Ben.

"We'd better get back downstairs. I'm sure the gang is about ready to be fed," he said once he'd placed the sword back in its place.

"Thank you for sharing your passion with me, Ben."

"You bet."

I was enjoying myself more than I'd expected. Being near Ben was calming. He had such an immovable inner strength—I was drawn in. It wasn't the same energy I got from being around Mateo. I had only been with my husband for two years, but it felt as if I'd matured emotionally after the ordeal. I went into marriage as a child and emerged on the other side as an adult.

It was an odd thought.

I went to chat with Olivia once Ben and I were outside, but I kept an eye on our host. He interacted effortlessly with everyone. His laugh was sincere, and his personality seemed to attract everyone.

"He's quite something, isn't he?" Olivia said.

"Who?" I asked, pretending not to know who she was referring to.

"Dr. Forbes."

"Yeah, he's a good doctor."

"That's not all he is," she grinned.

"Settle down, you. It's the alcohol talking."

"Don't tell me you haven't thought of those skilled hands caressing your unmentionables."

"Okay, I think it's time we get some food into you, missy," I laughed.

"I know exactly what I need," she laughed, "and it ain't a burger."

Who could blame her? I guessed Ben was everything a woman could want. Sexy, smart, kind, and single. But I wasn't looking. I'd learned my lesson. I wasn't ready to have a man in my life. I wondered if I'd ever be ready again.

"Come and get it," Ben called once the meat was cooked.

He'd laid out quite a spread. Hungry mouths got involved and soon we were eating and laughing at Dave's amusing antics. I was having a good time for a change. I even laughed, which was something I didn't think I would ever do again, considering the shitshow that had been my life for so long.

I caught Ben every so often sneaking looks in my direction. Olivia wasn't making any bones about her attraction toward him, but he handled her advances with gentlemanly poise. Nothing is quite as determined as an inebriated resident doctor with a major crush on her mentor.

It was late when the party started to ebb. Ben had arranged a bus to and from his home, for those who wanted to drink alcohol. I thought that was rather thoughtful of him. I didn't opt in as I wasn't going to drink much, so I was the last one to leave.

"Barbeques at the Forbes mansion end up in quite a mess," I said as I looked around.

"Not to worry. I have cleaners coming in tomorrow morning."

"Thank goodness. I was going to offer to help clean up, but..."

"Dodged a bullet there," Ben laughed.

"I'd say. I'd better be on my way too. Thank you for a lovely day, Ben."

"It was my pleasure," he said. "I'll walk you out."

I fished around in my bag for the keys to a little runaround I'd bought the week before. It was a far cry from the Mercedes I'd gotten used to, but it got me where I wanted to go, and it ran on a sniff of an oil rag.

"Well, goodnight, Peyton."

"Goodnight, Ben."

Brief awkward silence. Ben bent down and kissed me. I was startled but I didn't move away. It wasn't an all-out, tongue aerobics kiss, but my spine tingled, nonetheless.

"Travel safely," he smiled.

"I will."

11

BEN

What was I thinking, kissing Peyton? And, that after I'd assured her that I wasn't going to bite. I hoped she wasn't offended, although, from the feel of her lips, she didn't seem to be. I'd gotten myself into a right mess, emotionally. I couldn't stop thinking about her.

Peyton was so unlike her fellow residents. She was streets ahead when it came to maturity, an attribute I found very attractive in a woman. I could tell that she was intelligent from the questions she asked and the way she held a conversation. I knew that she would be bolder in her personal life as her confidence returned. In my experience, browbeaten women, however intelligent they may be, were weary of coming out of their shells for fear of being rammed back inside by an abusive man.

I wondered who the bastard was that had pushed Peyton around. I had no time for men like that. I could only hope that someday his and my paths would cross so I could give him a taste of his own medicine.

I was invited to compete in an out-of-state, premier martial arts tournament. The event was coming up soon and I thought it would be nice if Peyton could experience what the discipline was all about—seeing as she'd shown such interest in it at the barbeque. So, I decided to invite her along.

I had to be careful how I did it though. The last thing she needed was a man looking to take advantage of her. That was not my intention. The truth was that I enjoyed her company. Sure, I'd be lying to myself if I didn't at least admit that the attraction was ridiculously strong, but I'd take it slow—give her time to get to know me better.

"Good morning, team," I greeted the eager residents when I arrived at the hospital. "Let's do our rounds, shall we?"

About half an hour later, after we'd seen all the patients and gone through the medical details of their recuperation, pain management, and such, I asked Peyton if I could have a quick word with her before I left to see my private patients at my private practice.

"Sure, Ben. What's up?"

"I'm attending a big martial arts tournament in two weeks, and I wondered if you'd like to come along. I thought you might enjoy it as you seemed quite interested when I showed you my dojo."

I couldn't read Peyton's expression, so I added a bit of reassurance.

"No funny business, I promise. We'll stay in separate accommodations."

She chewed on her bottom lip before she answered.

"Uh, yeah. That sounds like fun, actually. I'd love to go."

"Great. I know you're going to enjoy it. I'll see you tomorrow."

"Thanks, Ben."

Was my smile too bright? I was sure it was like that of a teenager who'd scraped together the courage to ask the prettiest girl to the prom, and she said yes.

Leave before you say something stupid, Ben.

What the hell had gotten into me?

* * *

"That was absolutely brutal!"

Peyton's face was lit up and her smile was genuinely infectious.

"You are brilliant. I thought for sure that guy was going to run away and cower in the corner of the room."

"Stop, I'm blushing," I laughed.

"No, seriously. Well done."

"Thank you, but that was only the first fight. Plenty more to come. I may still need a stretcher."

"Oh, I don't believe that for a second."

Peyton and I were having a drink between my scheduled fights. We'd arrived a day before the tournament so that I could have a few sessions with my trainer, Dylan, before the event.

Dylan was a very accomplished martial arts instructor, who'd lived and trained with the best in Japan. He was exceptionally knowledge-able when it came to technique, but I enjoyed his spiritual take on life even more than his skill as a trainer. He was a deep thinker, and in all the years that he'd been my mentor, I'd never once seen him lose his cool. Not that he was a pushover, mind you.

"How many more?" Peyton asked.

"What? Sport fights?"

"Is that what it's called?"

"Yes, when you fight in a tournament it counts for points. That's called sport fighting. Otherwise, it's sparring. Or, if you're fighting for your life or self-defense, then it's called Budo."

"Hhmm."

I could see the gears turning over behind her bewitching eyes.

"What's going on in that head of yours Dr. Taylor?"

"I was just thinking that I'd like to dabble a bit in Budo. I reckon every woman needs to know how to defend herself."

"I agree. I'll be happy to show you a few moves if you like."

"That would be great, Ben. Thank you."

"Anytime. In the meanwhile, I'd better get back to the mat or I'll have to deal with Dylan. And, trust me, ain't nobody got time for that," I smirked.

"Yeah, I'd hate to get on the wrong side of any karate yogi."

"Sensei," I chuckled.

"Yup, him either."

Peyton was so bloody cute.

The rest of the day went well, better than I'd expected. Throughout the next two days, I made my way, steadily, up the victor's ladder, and by the end of the competition, I was on top. I couldn't have been prouder of my victory. I'd come away with a beautiful trophy and one or two bruises, but nothing I couldn't handle.

The only thing I'd grappled with and fought hard against was not sneaking into Peyton's room at night to make love to her. I lay in my room at night, fantasizing about touching her silky skin and kissing her perfect lips. It was such a shame to leave her beauty unappreciated.

I wasn't at all surprised when Peyton asked me to teach her how to defend herself. I was going to make damn sure that she'd be more than able to take care of herself the next time anyone tried to push her around.

"We have a day or two before we have to be back at the hospital," I said when we were on our way home. "Would you like me to show you a few moves in the meantime?"

"I'd like that."

"Okay. I'll drop you at home so you can unpack and freshen up. Shall I fetch you tomorrow morning?"

"I'll come to you. What time?"

"Will 10 am work for you?"

"Yup. I'll see you then."

I wanted to say, it's a date, but that was cringeworthy and cheesy, so I smiled and nodded instead.

* * *

"Good morning, Sensei," Peyton said and bowed when I opened the door.

She was wearing sweatpants, sneakers, and a T-shirt, and her hair was tied back into a ponytail.

"Ohayō, kohai," I said and bowed in return. "I see someone has been brushing up on her old karate movies."

"Hai, sensei," she said, extenuating the 'h' for effect.

"Cute."

"Alrighty, Ben Forbes, let's see if you can make a ninja out of me," Peyton grinned and walked toward the dojo.

"Not sure if the world is ready for such a beautiful assassin."

"Well, that's just tough. I'm ready to learn, so the world better watch its ass."

"Spoken like a true newbie," I laughed.

Once inside the dojo, Peyton removed her sweatpants. She wore tights underneath. I nearly swallowed my tongue when I saw the perfect curves of her backside. She'd always been in scrubs or loose-fitting jeans. There wasn't much hiding one's figure in tights.

"Ready?" I asked as she moved onto the mat.

"Ready."

I showed her the basics of how to stand and block blows first.

"Well, this seems fairly straightforward. What? No wax on wax off?" she smirked.

"You'll get there," I grinned and swept her legs out from under her.

Peyton went down like a sack of potatoes. Flat on her back.

"Hey! That was mean. I wasn't ready," she laughed.

I reached out to help her up, but Peyton had other ideas. She swiped at my legs as soon as she had a grip on my hand. I wasn't expecting it, plus I was cracking up, so I stumbled and fell halfway on top of her.

Peyton thought it was the funniest.

"Please. I've got the measure of this karate thing without breaking a sweat," she laughed.

"Oh, really? Let's see you get out of this?" I teased and held her hands above her head.

"Okay. That's dirty play," she said, staring into my eyes.

"I could let you go, of course. But you don't know the magic word, do you?"

I was so hard by now it was uncomfortable. Peyton's hair smelled so damn good, and her skin felt smooth and warm under mine.

"Open sesame?'" she grinned.

"Nope," I said and brought my face closer to hers. "Try again."

"Hocus pocus?"

"Wrong again," I said, my breathing racing as I stopped just short of our lips touching.

She opened her mouth to speak again, but I stopped her by placing my lips over hers. I kissed her passionately, shifting my body slightly so that she could feel my erection against her thigh.

I expected Peyton to resist me or push me away, but she didn't. I knew enough about body language to know that she wanted me just as much as I wanted her, so I let go of her wrists and ran my hands down her sides. She broke out in goosebumps.

Peyton's nipples were hard under her crop top. I couldn't resist them, so I slipped my hand under the top and moved her breast free before I took the nipple into my mouth.

Peyton moaned as I did so. We were breathing hard now. I slipped my hand down the inside of her thigh and back up again. She quivered at my touch which only made me more determined to get her naked.

"You are so sexy," I whispered and slid my hand into her pants.

Her core was swollen, warm, and wet. Peyton moaned as I moved my fingers around her clit, massaging every inch of her gently, then a little faster. She moved her hips up and down to meet my fingers, hungry for release.

I stopped suddenly and pulled off her pants. Peyton opened her legs to allow me easy access to her womanly perfection. I covered her with my mouth, sucking hungrily, darting my tongue in and out of her swollen core.

There was a raw urgency to her that sent my head into a tailspin. I'd expected her to fight me, but instead, she pulled me in, deeper, harder.

I couldn't wait anymore, so I pulled myself free from my pants. My hungry lover grasped at my hard cock and stroked it passionately. She played her fingers over the tip of my penis and teased me until I thought I would explode into a thousand pieces.

I looked into her eyes as I thrust into her. Her mouth curved a little on one side as she welcomed into her. I found her hands and pressed them into the floor above her head. Peyton wrapped her legs around me and used her heels to time my thrusts.

I kissed her madly while we lay there, writhing in sweet passion. Her lips were sweet, and her tongue moved expertly as she explored every inch of my mouth.

"Come for me," I whispered as I buried my face into her neck.

She was close. I could feel the urgency in her movements. Peyton had a hunger inside of her that spoke volumes. Who had neglected this perfect creature? What man wouldn't treasure every ounce of her body and soul? What a fool! I wasn't going to make the same mistake. No. I planned on soaking up every little bit of passion and savoring the woman who lay underneath me, writhing in pleasure.

I let go of Peyton's wrists and as soon as I did, she grabbed my naked ass and dug her nails into my flesh. I slipped my hands under her perfect bottom and pulled her against me. Together we rode the wave until we crested.

Peyton let out a primal scream when she climaxed. It was wonderful. For a single moment, she'd forgotten where she was and that she'd been through trauma and let go.

My orgasm was long and intense. Our bodies shuttered and twitched together in perfect sync until they finally became perfectly still. Except for the racing of our hearts and our attempts at trying to catch our breath, Peyton and I lay perfectly still on the dojo floor.

"So," she finally said, "what's the magic word?"

"Who the hell can remember after an orgasm like that?" I chuckled. "I vote we use that rather than a magic word."

"Can't argue that" she laughed.

"I don't know about you, Dr. Taylor, but I'm no longer in the mood for karate."

"I agree. I don't suppose there's any food left from yesterday? I'm starving."

"You're in luck. I've got some ribeye in the fridge. I'm sure we can rustle up a salad to go with it."

"Who needs salad? Let me at that meat, Doc."

"Dearest, Peyton. You are fast becoming my favorite training buddy," I laughed and reached for my clothes.

I kissed her before we got up.

"Lesson one complete," I said and bowed down once we were standing.

"Thank you, Sensei," she chuckled and bowed.

I walked behind Peyton and watched her cute ass as she moved.

Man! I've gotta get me some more of that!

What an absolutely brilliant start to my day.

12

PEYTON

hat have I done?

It had been a week since Ben, and I tore each other's clothes off in his dojo. Fortunately for me, he was away at a doctor's conference, so I wasn't forced to look him in the eye. God only knew what I was going to say to him when he got back.

Ben Forbes was arguably the best lover I'd ever had. Not that I've had scores, but he stood in a class of his own. Tender, receptive, insatiable…

Don't forget hung like a horse.

There was that. I had no idea penises could bend that way, but ho hum…lucky me. My stomach played leapfrog with my colon whenever I closed my eyes and replayed the passionate afternoon we'd spent together.

Of course, no good deed goes unpunished. I felt so guilty. I was a married woman after all. Not that I gave a rat's furry asshole about the fact that I'd cheated on Mateo—he didn't deserve my loyalty—but I felt bad because I had selfishly dragged Ben into my trainwreck of a life. He deserved better than that.

I wondered what Mateo would do if I sent him divorce papers. The mind boggles, I thought. For a start, I didn't trust him to know where I was, and secondly, Mateo Garcia would rather hunt me down and kill me than give me the satisfaction of signing a divorce decree. He as much as told me that when I tried to leave him the first time.

No. I'd have to keep that burden to myself. Ben didn't have to know, and I prayed to God that he would never find out about my psycho husband in Mexico. I would never live down the shame.

It was time to call home and find out if Mateo had been harassing my family. I called Mom.

"Sweetheart! How are you?"

"Hi, Mom. I'm good. How about you?"

"Fine, thanks. Missing you, though. I wish we could see you. You feel as far away as Mexico still."

"I know. I hate not seeing you. It won't be forever, Mom. How's Dad?"

"He's fine. Out walking."

"Glad to hear it. I don't suppose that was entirely his idea."

"How perceptive of you," Mom chuckled. "How are you really, Peyton? Dad and I worry about you."

"Well, stop that right now. I'm fine. Work is keeping me busy, so no complaints. How's Madi's pregnancy coming along?"

"You know your sister. She's glowing."

"I'm so glad."

"How are you feeling, sweetheart? Are you still in pain?"

I knew my mother was referring to my miscarriage. She'd been so excited when I told her I was pregnant. It must have been a shock when I told her she wasn't going to have another grandbaby. That was an area within which she excelled. Millicent Taylor was a doting grandmother.

"I'm doing great, Mom. No pain."

"Thank God for that."

"Mom, I'm worried that Mateo will come looking for me. You haven't seen him, have you? You would tell me, wouldn't you?"

"Of course, I would. No, Peyton. That son of a bitch won't show his face here. Not after what he's done. Your father will most certainly shoot him on the spot."

"Yeah, that's what I'm afraid of."

"How's your new job, darling?" Mom asked, ever the skilled focus shifter.

"It's great. I work with a fun bunch of doctors."

"How's Dr. Forbes? You mentioned he was the one who appointed you. Is he blown away by how smart my baby girl is?"

He's impressed with the way you move your hips when you're on top of him, that's for sure!

"Ben's well, thanks. He's a very good doctor. I'm learning a lot from him."

"Ben? A solid name. I knew a Ben once. What a gorgeous specimen he was."

"Wow. Hello, who is this? Where is Millie Taylor?"

"What? You think I was always a middle-aged woman?"

"Middle-aged? Are you planning on living until you're one-hundred-and-twenty?"

"Aren't you a cheeky monkey?" Mom laughed.

"Calling it as I see it, Millicent."

"Give it time. You'll be my age one day and you'll wonder why people are calling you ma'am when you still feel like a teenager."

"You're nuts, Ma. I love you."

"Love you too, baby."

After talking to my mother, I decided it was time to call Madison.

"Hi, Madi."

"Peyton. This is a nice surprise. How are you?"

"I'm okay, thanks. Just spoke to Mom. She says you're doing well."

"Actually, my left leg goes all numb every so often. Looks like the baby is lying on my sciatica nerve. Oh, Peyton, I'm sorry. I wasn't thinking."

"Please, Madison, don't apologize. It's okay. I'm so happy for you and Tom."

"It was such a shock, Peyton. How are you coping?"

"I'm okay. Most days I want to drive to Mexico and kick the shit out of Mateo. Other days I get through with minimal rage bubbling under."

"I don't know how you did it. I would have been a nervous wreck. You're very brave, Sis."

"I don't feel brave. I feel stupid and gullible."

"That's crazy. Mateo showed you a side of himself that he wanted you to see. Who really knows what goes on in anyone else's mind? People are more devious than we could ever imagine."

"Thank you for saying that, Madison."

"I'm sorry I wasn't there for you."

"You have a family and you put them first. That's the way it should be. Do you know the sex of the baby?"

"Yes, it's a girl. The boys aren't impressed. They're not sure about a sister being part of their 'gang'."

"Figures," I chuckled.

"If she's anything like you, her brothers had better watch out."

"Funny."

"How's your residency? Have you decided what to specialize in yet?"

"I'm toying with a few ideas. Surgery is definitely where it's at for me."

"I hope you cut better than you sew," Madison laughed.

"Hey, elementary school quilt class doesn't count."

"I'm sure your patients will be relieved to hear that. Mom still has all those disasters packed away in a box in the attic. Who knows what she's going to do with all that crap."

"She's probably saving it for when she needs leverage. Use it to torture us in front of our kids or something."

"I look forward to the day when you and I can watch our kids grow up together, Peyton."

"Me too."

I heard a noise in the background, and Madi yelling at one of her boys about playing inside the house with a ball.

"Damn it. I have to run. Sorry, Peyton. My vase just bit the dust and there's water and flowers all over the rug."

"Don't be too mad at them," I laughed.

"Too late. Love you, sis. Thanks for the chat."

"Love you too."

I imagined my sister rushing to the scene of the crime while two little boys scarpered for the safety of an oak tree.

My conversation with Madi was different from the norm. I felt a connection with her I'd never had before. Perhaps one changes when one's had a baby inside you. It seemed to soften me. I couldn't explain it without sounding like a tree hugger, but there was most certainly something softer in me. Loss is the great leveler.

What was Mateo up to? He was too quiet. I was sure he'd march into my parents' home and demand to know where I was. Then again, the man was a coward. Only a coward would abuse and kill women.

I had spoken to Lula only once since I left Mexico, and I wondered how she was. I missed Lula. She was a wonderful friend to me when I had no one to talk to. I dialed her cell number.

"Hey, girl. How are you?"

"Peyton! Hi!"

"Sorry I haven't called in a while. How are you, Lula?"

"Good. How are you? Are you okay?"

"I'm fine."

"How's the baby?"

"I lost the baby."

"Mierda," she said softly. "I'm so sorry, my friend."

"Thank you."

"Fuck that man! I have a good mind to inject him with a cocktail of drugs he'll never recover from."

"Sounds heavenly, but don't you do that to yourself. It's alright, Lula. I'm okay. Honestly, it's probably for the best. No child deserves a father like Mateo."

"No, but they sure deserve a mother as fine as you, Peyton."

"What a lovely thing to say. Thank you."

"He's been here twice, you know."

"What?!"

"Uh-huh. I wondered what he'd say if I told him I knew the truth about him. The fucking slimeball."

"Oh, no. Don't you dare, Lula. He's dangerous. He won't hesitate to harm you. He's a cunning fucking coward which makes him unpredictable."

"Yeah? Well, I have drug knowledge on my side. He must come. It will be the last thing he ever does."

"Promise me you won't engage with him, Lula. Promise!"

"Fine. I promise."

"What did he want?"

"He played the broken husband card. Said it was all a big misunderstanding and that he misses you terribly, blah blah, blah. I didn't tell him anything. As far as he knows, I know nothing about nothing."

"Good. Keep it that way."

"I have news, but now I'm not sure I want to tell you."

"What is it, Lula?"

"I'm pregnant."

"Oh, Lula! That's wonderful news. I'm so happy for you. Ángel must be so excited."

"Yes, he keeps talking to my stomach as if the kid can hear him. He bought a baseball mitt, so I asked him what he was going to do if it was a girl. He said he doesn't mind what the sex of the baby is. The two of them are going to play baseball no matter what."

"Ah, that's so sweet. You've got yourself a good one there, my friend."

"I know. I'm so happy. Hang on. Are you working?"

"That's right. I haven't told you yet. I'm completing my residency. The doctor who performed the DNC offered me a job."

"That's amazing. Is he a good guy?"

"He is."

"Is he cute?"

"Very."

"Hmm."

"I know what you're thinking, and you can stop scheming. I'm married and he doesn't need my drama in his life."

"Sounds like I hit a nerve," Lula giggled.

"No. No nerve. I'm just being practical. Besides, it will be a very long time before I trust a man again."

"Don't do that, Peyton."

"Do what?"

"Don't assume the worst just because Mateo is a rotten apple. Don't close yourself off to the possibility of love and a family."

"I'm not, but it's too soon to think about love. Besides, I don't know if I'll ever trust a man again. I don't trust myself to choose well either."

"You're smart. You'll pull it off."

"I have to go, Lula. I'll call again soon. I promise."

"Be careful, Peyton. Look after yourself."

"I will."

I was happy for Lula and Ángel. My friend's husband was a sweetheart. She'd chosen well.

I checked the time. It was getting late, and I hadn't eaten yet. I was on the night shift for two weeks. I was glad because Ben seldom came around during the night shift unless he had to perform an emergency C-section.

But was I really glad? I missed him. I didn't think I would. Then again, I hadn't imagined I'd sleep with him either. So much for not getting involved with another man.

The problem was that Ben was the sort of person who was almost impossible to stay away from. He drew me in like a magnet. I'd caught myself a few times on the brink of telling him everything. Especially while I lay in his arms after we'd been intimate.

No, Peyton. Remember, you're doing this to keep him safe. If he knows about Mateo, he'll do something about it. That's who Ben is. He cannot know!

The voice inside my head was right. If I wanted to keep Ben safe, I'd have to keep my mouth shut. And that was exactly what I was going to do.

13

BEN

It was good to be back in New York. I'd had my fill of traveling around when I was in the military. Doing it for a work conference here and there was doable, but I had a feeling that was my limit.

I hadn't seen Peyton since we had sex, but I thought about her constantly. How was I going to get closer to her? When we'd made love, it was clear that she was cautious with her soul even though she had been generous with her body. It was almost as if she'd been ashamed or embarrassed.

Whatever her last lover had done to her must have left emotional as well as physical scars. What happened to Peyton?

I found her, hard at work, at the hospital on Friday morning. I stood quietly in the corner, watching her as she spoke to a patient. I loved watching her when she wasn't aware of me. She seemed more at ease when no one was looking.

"Oh! Ben," she said when she turned around and saw me standing in the doorway. "Hi."

"Hello, Dr. Taylor," I smiled warmly.

"Dr. Forbes," she smiled. "How was your trip?"

"Very informative. What have the mice been up to whilst the cat's been away?"

"The usual."

"How's Mrs. Riley doing?"

"She passed on Tuesday."

"I'm sorry to hear that. How is her son?"

"Heartbroken, but he didn't try to resus, so that's something."

"Indeed. Well done, Peyton."

"Thank you, Ben."

"Would you like to have dinner with me?"

Peyton nibbled briefly on her lower lip. I stood, silently, while I waited for her to weigh up the pros and cons in her head. It felt like an eternity before she answered me.

"Sure. That will be nice."

"Okay. I'll call you later."

Peyton smiled and mission-walked to perform whatever task was next on her to-do list.

* * *

"You look beautiful."

"Thank you. I thought I'd wear a dress."

"You look good in a dress," I grinned. "Almost as good as you do naked."

"Steady on, Doc," she blushed.

"Sorry, but I couldn't resist. What would you like to drink? Wine? Tequila?"

"Oh, what the hell. I haven't been out for a while, so I think tequila is a good call. As long as you promise not to take advantage of me."

"Would I do such a diabolical thing to my favorite resident?"

Peyton laughed. She was even more beautiful when she was relaxed. I wanted to get up from my chair and kiss her, but I resisted the urge.

"Good evening. Welcome to Shana's Streak Ranch. What can I get you to drink?"

"Hi, Alice," I greeted the waitress. "What tequila do you stock?"

"We have quite a few, Sir."

Alice rambled on about blue agave and the like, so I turned my gaze to Peyton, who clearly knew more about the cheeky cactus than I.

"Patrón Añejo will be fine, thanks," Peyton answered.

"Make those two doubles," I said.

"I think you're going to enjoy this," Peyton smiled when the golden, honey-colored tipple arrived at the table.

"Do I throw it back and lick salt from your neck?" I grinned.

"Don't you dare. This cheeky liquid is to be savored. There will be no chugging the Patrón Añejo tonight," she winked. "But it's interesting to see how your mind works, Dr. Forbes."

"You have no idea, Dr. Taylor."

I was itching to know more about her past, but the smart money was on donning kit gloves. I couldn't exactly come out and ask her what the hell had happened to make her so cautious, so I decided to try another approach. I'd tell Peyton about myself and hope she would feel comfortable enough to share her story with me.

"My brother on the other hand, well, he's the tequila baby of the family."

"Oh? Tell me more."

"Owen is the rogue of the family. I've always been the sensible one. I guess that's what happens when you're the firstborn. Although, I must say, since he met the love of his life, he's been rather, dare I say, normal?"

"Is he married?"

"No. He and his girlfriend, Suzanna, have been together for about two years now."

"Do you guys get along? You and she, I mean."

"Yes, Suzy's a lovely person. Her mother on the other hand. Wow! I would wish her on my worst enemy."

"It's true what they say. You can't choose your family."

"Spoken like someone who has experience," I nudged ever so gently. "Do you have siblings?"

"An older sister."

"Are you guys close?"

"We get along fine. She's older."

"Is she also in the medical field?"

Peyton chuckled.

"Madison? No. She's a committed mom and home executive."

"Okay."

The conversation felt a bit like pulling teeth. But I now knew that Peyton had a sister, and that was a good start.

"Have you always wanted to be a doctor?" she asked.

"Oh, yes. There were two things I always knew I wanted to do. One is medicine and the other martial arts."

"How did you end up in the military?"

"A good friend from school called me up one day and told me that his unit was looking for a doctor. I had just finished my residency and a career in the armed forces appealed to my sense of patriotism. I guess when you're in your twenties, it's an exciting prospect."

"Do you miss it?"

"I miss the people."

"Where were you stationed?"

"All over the show. Afghanistan was my last stint. I knew after that I needed to be home with my family."

Come on, Peyton. Take the bait. Tell me more.

"So, what were you like as a kid?" I asked when my dinner date stopped talking.

"Quiet."

"Stop! I can't believe that."

"Thanks for that. Am I really such a talker now?"

"No," I laughed. "That's not what I meant. You just don't strike me as a wallflower."

"Oh, I wasn't. Not by a long shot. But I was a careful child. That changed as soon as puberty hit. That was when I found my voice and came into my own."

"How do you find the Big Apple?" I asked as I didn't want to make it obvious to Peyton that I was on a bit of a fishing expedition.

"It's busy."

"Yup. There is that."

"I like it. I love my job. Thank you, Ben."

"I must thank you. So far, the hospital is the winner. You're a good doctor."

"Do you say that to all the young residents who happen to cross your dojo mat?"

"Ouch."

"Sorry. That was mean. I didn't mean that to sound the way it did."

"Well, if you must know, my pretty little viper, you are the first resident who has ever seen the inside of my dojo...and my Katsumi."

"Okay. You've successfully reprimanded me. My bad."

"I'm not in the habit of seducing my students, Peyton. It's important to me that you know that."

"What are you saying, Ben?"

"What I'm saying, you stunning creature, is that I'm truly interested in you. I'm not playing a game."

"I appreciate your candor, Ben."

"But?"

Peyton was squirming in her seat. The last thing I wanted was for her to feel uncomfortable.

"I'm not ready. Honestly, I don't know when I will be."

"Take as much time as you need, Peyton. I'm not going anywhere."

* * *

"I see you mean business today," Owen said when I hauled out the ten-weight fishing rod.

It was Sunday morning, and I was pondering my situation with Peyton. I thought that dinner had gone as well as I could have expected. The beautiful young doctor had opened up a crack wide enough for me to slip one foot into. I planned on wriggling that foot until the crack widened.

"What's up with you today?" Owen asked me.

"Why?"

"You're grinning like a fox, and I've asked you the same question three times without success. Hello! Are you in there, Ben? What am I missing, Bro?"

"You mean, what have I been missing?"

"Aaah. I see. Looks like my brother has found himself a woman. I told you being a gynecologist is like shooting fish in a barrel, Dr. Forbes. Who is she?"

"Her name is Dr. Peyton Taylor."

"Smart. Keep it in the same income bracket," Owen chuckled. "Tell me about her. How did you meet? Or is that a stupid question?"

"She was a patient of mine."

"Was? Did she report you for creepy behavior? Where exactly did you stick that light of yours, Doc?"

"Wouldn't you like to know?" I laughed. "I performed a DNC on her after she lost her baby."

"I don't mean to come across as an alarmist, Ben, but it sounds like this could be a tricky situation. Are you sure you're being wise? Where's the father of the baby?"

"Wherever he is, he'd be wise to stay there. You should have seen her, Owen. She was quite a mess internally. I don't know what happened, but I suspect she didn't fall down a flight of stairs because she's clumsy."

"Obviously, I haven't met her, so I don't have all the facts, but is this a good idea, Ben? I don't want to see you get hurt."

"That's sweet of you, little brother, but I'll be fine. Trust me. Peyton is worth the effort."

"What do you know about Peyton?"

"She's very intelligent, clearly resilient, and I'm crazy about her."

"Have you inspected her post-operative work yet?"

"Cute."

"I thought so. You're not the only bowfin in the family."

"As a matter of fact, none of your business, you nosy reprobate."

"Hmmm. Well, blow me down. You must really like this girl."

"I just wish I could get her to open up to me a little more. Peyton is very guarded."

"If what you suspect about the father of her dead child is correct, she has cause to be. And so, may I add, should you be. You don't know the extent of the mess she's left behind."

"I appreciate the sentiment, but I can take care of myself."

"Of course, you can. But I'm not talking about physically. I mean emotionally. What if she goes back to him? Abused women have a habit of doing that. God knows why."

"Peyton doesn't strike me as that kind of woman. She's tough."

"I hope so. For both your sakes."

"Are we gonna stand around all day, or are we gonna catch a big ass bass?"

"Okay, but I'm warning you. Loser buys dinner and drinks."

"You're on."

I knew Owen was right. I was being less than smart to get involved with a woman without knowing the facts.

It's way too late for contemplating the facts, Ben. You're in it now, whether it's a dumb idea or not.

No matter who or what Peyton had run from, I had made up my mind to be there for her. I would keep my curiosity in check until she was ready to share her past with me. I wasn't going to let her down the way she had been let down already. Peyton was worth so much more than that.

Owen caught one of the biggest largemouth bass I'd ever seen. The little shit crowed all the way to the restaurant and throughout dinner. The more beer he had, the bigger the fish tale.

I dropped him at home just before 11 pm. I was exhausted. It had been a long week and I was ready to hit the hay. After a warm shower, I lay in bed and thought about what my brother had said.

Was I being a fool? Would I fall in love with Peyton just to see her leave and go back to her ex?

I found my phone in the dark and typed a message to the woman who had captivated me.

Hey, Doc. See you in the morning. Sleep tight.

14

PEYTON

"I miss you, Pey. Can't I come and see you?" Alyssa begged.

"No, Lyss, it's not safe. What if Mateo follows you? He could have someone watching you. I can't risk it. I'm sorry."

"Fucking prick. This is insane! I can't go for the rest of my life knowing I'm never going to see you again. There must be something we can do. Come on. We're smart women."

I thought about it for a minute. Alyssa was right. Mateo had taken enough from me. Why the hell was I allowing him to take more?

"Okay. Give me a few days to think about it and I'll get back to you."

"Fine. But you'd better think fast. If I can't see you, I swear I'm going to fly to Mexico City and put a bullet between that fucker's eyes. I mean it, Peyton."

"Are you feeling better now, Rambo?" I chuckled.

"A little," she laughed.

"I know this is frustrating. Imagine how I feel. I miss you all so much and I haven't had an opportunity to be with Madison through this pregnancy."

"I'm sorry, Peyton. I'm ranting on. I'm being selfish."

"No. You're not. You're right. Mateo has taken enough. We won't let him take any more. I'll call you in a few days. I promise."

"Chat soon. Love you."

"I love you too."

I hung up and made my way to the shower. It had been a long shift and all I wanted to do was to put my feet up and veg in front of the TV with wine and a pizza.

I had just washed my hair and was dripping water all over the bathroom floor because I forgot that the clean towels were in the laundry basket in the kitchen. Annoyed with myself, I tiptoed, naked, to the kitchen and grabbed a bath towel.

I nearly fainted when I heard a knock on the kitchen window. Ben was standing there with a gigantic grin on his face. I wrapped myself in the towel before I opened the door.

"Wow. Best greeting ever," he smirked. "You're lucky that was me and not your landlord."

"What can I say? I wasn't expecting company," I laughed, feeling foolish.

"No kidding."

Ben had the same look in his eyes as he had when he flopped on top of me in the dojo. It was the look of a man who wanted me. No woman ever confused that look with something inconsequential. I was suddenly very aware of my nakedness under the towel—and very turned on.

Ben closed the door behind him and moved purposefully toward me. I knew what he was thinking. No words were needed, as his eyes were doing all the talking. I walked slowly backward until I ran out of floor space. My back was against the wall and my aroused lover had no intention of halting his advance.

My inner thighs were tingling, and a swollen, throbbing heat settled in my groin. Ben took a strand of my wet hair and rubbed it gently between his fingers. I stood perfectly still. With his free hand, he reached for the knot in the towel and slowly untied it. My covering dropped to the floor with a fluffy thud. I was bare ass naked, still wet in places where the material hadn't drawn away the moisture from my shower.

My lover's eyes hungrily roamed my body. Without a word, he took my left nipple into his warm mouth. I moaned softly at the delicate touch of his tongue. Ben moved away and looked into my eyes. Was he asking for permission?

I reached out and unbuttoned his shirt. I ran my hands over his taught torso, moving steadily downwards to the prize. He let out a deep sigh when I reached into his pants and found his erection. The tip of his penis was wet, and I glided my finger around in a circle, teasingly.

Ben hastily took off his pants. We were both naked. I dropped to my knees in front of him and took him into my mouth. Ben plaited his fingers through my hair, arching his back as I moved my mouth rhythmically to and fro.

My lover was as hungry for me as I was for him. The way he picked me up suddenly and drove his cock into me was a dead giveaway. The heat of his penis filled me with pleasure. We made love in a frenzy until we were spent.

That night, after Ben had left, I had to admit to myself, once and for all, that I was in love with the handsome man who had once again brought me to orgasm. Okay. Twice.

* * *

"Okay. I've got it."

"Well, thank the daisies," Alyssa answered.

"People are always asking us if we're sisters. Right?"

"Right," she said slowly.

"What if I travel on your social security number? No one will be suspicious. That way, I can book a flight, and no one will be the wiser. I doubt whether Mateo is watching all the flights around The States. That's nearly impossible."

"Brilliant!"

"I told you I'd make a plan."

"When are you coming?"

"I have two weeks leave coming up in a few days. I'll come to you then. Don't tell my family. I want to surprise them. Also, if they don't know, they can't unwittingly do something to alert Mateo."

"Mum's the word."

* * *

Alyssa clung to me like a spider monkey baby to its mother.

"I can't believe it's really you, Pey. I've missed you so much."

The tears streaming down my cheeks had somehow rendered me speechless. We stood like that in her living room for the longest time. I'd disguised myself as soon as the plane landed. I wore a ridiculously oversized hoodie, baggy jeans, loud sneakers, and a duffle bag over my shoulder. I was sure that not even my mother would have recognized me.

"You look like a boy band reject," Alyssa laughed once she'd let go of me. "Did screaming young girls ask you for your autograph?"

"No, but it's never too late to change my profession."

"It's so good to see you. You look great. Under all that hoodie, I mean."

"I can't wait to get out of this getup. I look ridiculous."

I changed into something less androgynous while Alyssa poured us a drink.

"Here you go," she said and handed me a glass of wine.

"Bless your cotton socks. This is going to go down like a homesick mole."

"Cheers! To boy bands!"

"I'll drink to that."

"Are you hungry, Pey?"

"No, thanks. I had cardboard eggs and box juice on the plane."

"Ooh, first-class fair, hey."

"It's all I could afford on my almost-doctor budget," I grinned. "Lyss, I was thinking. It's better for my folks to come here, rather than for me to go to their place. What do you think?"

"I agree. Shall I call them and arrange it?"

"That would be great."

"Sure thing. Tomorrow, okay?"

"Of course. You and I have some serious catching up to do first."

"We do. Speaking of catching up, I think it's time you told me about Ben, don't you?"

I wasn't sure how to negotiate the very delicate subject with the one person who knew me too well.

"Oh, my giddy aunt! You're sleeping with him. Come on, I dare you to tell me I'm wrong."

"Ugh! That's what I get for flying all the way over here so you can interrogate me face-to-face. It's my own fault."

"You know I can always spot a lie in your eyes. It's easy to fib over the phone."

"I guess so. And, in answer to your question, yes."

"Good for you!"

"I'm not shouting it from the rooftops just yet, Lyss. I feel guilty as hell, to be honest."

"What the hell for? You don't owe Mateo a damn thing."

"It's not Mateo. I couldn't care less about him. I feel terrible because I'm keeping the truth from Ben. He's such an amazing guy, Lyss. I don't want to see him hurt."

"Have you told him anything?"

"No. Truthfully, I'm finding it very difficult to trust any man. Even Ben. I feel so vulnerable. I know Ben is different. But I also thought Mateo was special."

"You can't lose your trust in humanity because of one psychopath, Pey. If you do that, you'll never find love."

"I'm not sure I believe in love anymore."

"Oh, balls! That's crap and you know it. This isn't you, Peyton."

"Fuck," I sighed and rested my head in my hands. "I'm so confused."

"What is it, Peyton? I have a feeling you're not telling me the whole story."

Alyssa's question brought me to a scary crossroads. Did I dare to tell her the whole story about Mateo? It frightened me. There would be no going back once the truth was out there.

"Please, Pey. Talk to me."

"Okay. You're right. I haven't told you everything. If I do, you have to swear to me, Alyssa, and I mean swear to me, that you won't do anything stupid. You need to keep this to yourself. I'll implode if anything happens to you."

"Bloody hell, Peyton. What is it?"

"Promise me."

"Fine, I promise."

"I didn't leave Mateo just because he was abusive. It's far scarier than that. I left him because he's a murderer."

"What!"

Alyssa's face grew pale.

"What are you talking about?"

"Turns out I'm not the first Mrs. Garcia, either."

Alyssa stood up and headed for the kitchen.

"Hold on. I have a feeling we're going to need something stronger than wine for this," she said and came back with a bottle of tequila and two shot glasses.

"Okay," she said once she'd poured each of us a shot, "go ahead."

"I'm Mateo's third wife."

"Third! What happened to the other two? I can't believe he didn't tell you about them."

"There's a good reason for that. He didn't tell me because they're both dead."

"Fuck me," Alyssa whispered.

"Technically, they're missing. But I know they're dead."

"How? Did he tell you?"

"Not exactly. I discovered their dismembered bodies in freezers in the basement of our home when Mateo threw me down the flight of stairs."

Alyssa didn't say a word. She was so pale I thought she'd faint any moment. Then, her eyes welled up with tears before she came over to where I sat and threw her arms around me. She held me while she cried.

"I'm so sorry, Pey. I can't imagine how afraid you must have been. I can't believe I came so close to losing you," she cried as she clung to me.

"I've never been so scared in my life, Lyss," I said with a shaky voice. "I thought for sure I was going to die. Mateo had every intention of murdering me. You should have seen the look in his eyes just before he pushed me down those stairs."

"But, why? Why did he kill his wives? Why would a man do that?"

"Because we all dared to fall pregnant."

"Are you joking?"

"I wish I was. I'm serious. Mateo hates children."

"What the fuck! So, why doesn't he just have a vasectomy? That's the logical thing to do. Surely."

"Who the hell knows what goes on in the mind of a narcissistic psychopath? All I know is that I have to stay as far away from that man as humanly possible."

"Have you told your family?"

"No. I was afraid to. But I think it's time they knew. I'll tell them tomorrow. I'm going to need your help in keeping my father calm, Lyss. If Dad goes after Mateo, he will die. Of that, I'm one thousand percent sure."

"Why didn't you go to the police? Surely, the bodies are the proverbial smoking gun."

"Yeah. Unless the police chief is your bestie."

"What a fucking mess."

"No shit."

15

BEN

Peyton was back from her holiday. She hadn't told me much about where she was going before she left. To be fair, I supposed it was none of my business, really. But she was back, and I felt a whole lot more relaxed. I had an inexplicable knot in my stomach while she was away. I was convinced that the unease had a lot to do with the fact that I knew very little about her past.

My fear was that the woman over whom I'd become so protective would encounter the man who had abused her. Not that I was afraid she'd do something crazy like go back to him. No, I had a feeling Peyton had learned her lesson where he was concerned. I was worried because I knew that abusers weren't likely to let go of their prey without a fight.

"Wanna go fishing?" I called and asked her early one morning when I knew she wasn't working.

"Fishing? Really?"

"Uh-huh. It sounds nerdish, I know. But, once the fishing bug has bitten, it's hard to resist."

"Uhm…okay. I'll give it a shot."

"Great. I'll fetch you in an hour."

"What do I wear?"

"Something comfy. I'll gear you up."

"Ooh, pimp my fishing buddy," she giggled.

"You're going to be a pro by the time I'm done with you."

"Speaking of 'pro', I'm ready for a proper karate lesson when you are."

"Oh, yeah. I owe you one, don't I?"

"A lesson. Yes."

"It's not my fault, you know. You started it."

"What?" she laughed. "How did I start it?"

"You were all sexy and totally doable in that dojo mat," I chuckled.

"Okay, let's call it a tie. See you in an hour."

The mere thought of Peyton, naked and moaning in my arms, got me hot. I quickly put the image out of my mind and packed the fishing gear into my car. I made a few calls to patients before I drove over to pick up my new fishing buddy.

"I hope this is okay," Peyton said and pointed to her outfit.

"Yup, that will do the trick."

"I'm not going to reek of fish guts when today is over, am I?"

I laughed at the look on her face.

"You're a doctor. Surely, the smell of fish guts isn't the worst you've ever encountered?"

"Oh, good. So, you brought scrubs and gloves, did you?" she smirked.

"I have something better," I said and pulled out the chest wader and wading boots I'd packed for her.

"Had that lying around in the garage, did you?"

"A good fisherman is always prepared."

"Exactly how deep into the river are you planning on luring me dressed in that monkey suit?"

"Jump in, worry wart. I'll get you back home in one piece."

"Oh, I'm not worried."

"Good."

I reached over and pushed play on the CD. A song sprang to life. I watched Peyton out of the corner of my eye as she listened to the lyrics of the song.

"What are we listening to?" she hollered with laughter.

"I thought Craig Campbell's 'Fish' would get us in the mood," I laughed. "What do you think?"

"Oh, it's official. You're crazy," she said through her laughter.

"You better believe it."

By the time we arrived at the fishing spot, Peyton and I had learned the words to the song and belted out the chorus. It was wonderful seeing her so relaxed. Her laughter was genuine, and she appeared more relaxed than I'd ever seen her.

"Okay, rookie. Time to suit up," I said once we'd parked and got out of the car.

I helped Peyton with the chest wader before she slid her feet into the wading boots.

"You look adorable," I said and kissed her on the cheek.

"Point me to where the big fish are," she chuckled.

"Slow down there, Doc. Have you tried fly fishing before?"

"No, but I've seen it on TV."

"We're going to start on the bank of the river first. If we just blunder into the water, we may frighten the bass away."

"But aren't the fish in the middle of the water?"

"You'd be surprised how many big ones I've caught from the bank. Don't worry, we'll wade in a bit later."

"Okay.

"Here. Let me show you how to put the fly on the hook."

"We're talking artificial fly here, are we?" Peyton asked with a scrunched-up nose.

"Yeah."

"Good. Bugs. Yuk."

"Be careful. Watch your fingers. The hook is very sharp."

"Yes, Dr. Forbes," she mocked.

"Careful. Cheeky pupils get wet."

I helped her to rig up her line and showed her how to cast.

"Okay. Ready?" I asked.

"Ready."

"Give the line some slack, then cast. Let me show you how. Watch me."

I showed her a few times and soon she had her fly on the water.

"Like this?"

"That's it. Look at you. You're a natural."

"Sweet talker," she smiled.

"No, I'm serious. I wouldn't be at all surprised if you catch a fish before I do."

"Loser pays for dinner?" she grinned.

"Okay, I'll bite."

"Haha."

Less than an hour later, Peyton pulled her first bass out of the river.

"I feel as if I've been hustled," I laughed when she gave me a pleased grin.

"What can I say? You've got me hooked on fishing."

"Guess I walked straight into that one."

"Chest wader and all, Doc."

"You know you have to clean and eat what you catch, right?"

"Oh, no. I'll have a steak dinner, thanks."

* * *

My relationship with the beautiful Peyton was progressing nicely. I adored her sense of humor and we had so much in common. Still, there was a part of her that she kept inaccessible. I wondered if she'd ever let me in. Even when we made love, I could sense that she held back. She was a very sexy lover, for sure, but Peyton never surrendered to me fully.

I decided to drop by her apartment, unannounced one evening after work. My car was in the shop for maintenance and repairs, so I was in the shop's car. As I drove up, I saw Peyton getting into her car. She looked upset. I wondered what was wrong, so I decided, on a whim, to follow her.

I kept a good distance behind so that she wouldn't see me. I did feel a little guilty for spying on my girlfriend, but who could blame me?

How else would I ever learn more about the woman I was madly in love with? Was it a dick move? Probably.

Where was she going? I didn't recognize the area she was heading for. All kinds of scenarios mulled about inside my mind. I wished I knew why she was hiding things from me. Was she afraid that I would turn out to be the same kind of man as her ex? Couldn't Peyton tell how I felt about her from the way that I made love to her?

Her car crossed through an intersection. I was two cars behind her, and the light was about to turn red, so I sped up and passed the car ahead of me. It was a bit of a close call, I had to admit.

Nice one, Ben. How will it look if you cause an accident? You're a doctor, not Magnum P.I. Be careful, you fool.

Peyton suddenly sped up. I was struggling to keep up with her. What the hell was she doing? She was driving so recklessly; I decided to try and pull up next to her so I could tell her to slow down.

But the closer I came to her, the faster she drove. Was she trying to lose me? What the hell was Peyton doing?

Out of the corner of my eye, I saw a woman with a shopping trolley, trying to cross the road. Peyton wasn't planning on stopping. She clearly hadn't spotted the woman. I pressed down hard on my car horn in the hopes that she would look my way.

That's when it all went horribly wrong. Peyton saw the woman with the trolley at the last second, slammed on the brakes, and veered off the road, straight into a tree.

"Peyton!" I screamed as I saw her car coming to a sudden stop.

"Oh, fuck!" I yelled and pulled off the road.

I ran to her car as quickly as I could, while dialing 911 on my cell phone.

I flung open the car door and checked her vitals. Peyton was out cold. She had a gash on her forehead, and it looked to me as if she'd broken her arm. I prayed that she hadn't sustained internal injuries.

The ambulance arrived within ten minutes of my call. I explained to the paramedics what had happened and that I was a doctor, so they allowed me to ride with her in the back of the ambulance to the hospital.

I felt sick. What the fuck had I done? Why couldn't I have left well enough alone?

* * *

"Dr. Forbes, I'm Dr. Evans."

Dr. Evans was on call when we arrived at the ER. He was an orthopedic surgeon.

"Hi, Dr. Evans. Would you mind if I scrubbed in?"

"Not at all. Dr. Taylor has a fractured radius and a cracked ulna."

"No internal injuries?"

"Nothing showed up on the scan."

I followed him to the sink where we washed up before we entered the operating theater. I felt sick. I was sure I was as white as a sheet.

Dr. Evans had decided to operate on Peyton's arm as she would need it to be in tip-top shape for her job as a future surgeon. I appreciated his care and attention to detail. Once the operation was over, I stayed with her while she was in recovery.

I had no idea what I was going to tell her when she woke up. Nothing I could conjure up would be an excuse for my juvenile behavior. All I could do was hope that I hadn't blown it. Here she was, trying her best to move on from an abusive relationship, and what does her new boyfriend do? He scares her into an accident.

"What a fucking mess I've made of it," I mumbled under my breath while I stroked Peyton's lustrous hair. The gash in her forehead was neatly stitched and covered with a plaster. Dr. Evans had inserted a pin into her forearm to support the bone. He was sure that the injury would heal perfectly. I was grateful for that at least.

I watched as Peyton started to wake up. She was groggy when she opened her eyes. She looked confused for a moment as if she wasn't sure where she was or what had happened. She tried to sit up.

"Shhh…slowly. Don't get up," I urged her gently.

"Wha…Ben? Where am I? What happened?"

"You've been in an accident. You're in the recovery room."

"What?"

"It's okay. I'm here. You broke your arm, but other than that, you're going to be fine. You have no idea how lucky you are, Peyton."

She stared at me for a few moments before the light returned to her eyes.

"Wait. I remember now. Someone was following me. I crashed my car. How do you know? Did someone call you?"

You'd better tread carefully, Ben. Don't fuck this up.

16

PEYTON

I hated the after-effects of anesthesia. I tried my best to keep my eyes open but all I really wanted to do was close them and sleep for an eternity. My head was swimming, but I was happy to see Ben's face. I wondered how he managed to find me.

His soothing voice kept me calm. I'd wait until I stopped floating before I'd think about the possibility that Mateo had found me. Did he drive away when he saw the accident?

The sudden realization that he may be somewhere in the hospital scared me back to my senses. I sat up way too quickly. In hindsight, it was a silly thing to do because it made me instantly nauseous.

"Slowly, Peyton," Ben said again and gently rubbed my back. "You have a concussion."

"I'm gonna be sick," I said and heaved.

A bucket appeared before I could make good on my threat, and Ben rubbed my back while I threw up into the vessel. Great. Anesthesia *and* vomiting—super day.

"Ooph, my arm," I moaned once I stopped heaving.

"You fractured your radius and cracked the ulna. Dr. Evans did an excellent job of setting the broken bone. Don't worry, you'll heal quickly."

"What a mess. Ben, I have to get out of here."

He looked quizzically at me.

"What? I don't understand. You've just had surgery. You have to stay put for a bit."

"No. I can't. You don't understand. I have to leave. Right now!"

"Shhh. What's wrong, Peyton?"

Fuck! I wasn't ready to tell Ben about Mateo. Why did this have to happen? What would he say if he knew the truth?

"I think I'm in danger," I said softly, praying that Ben wouldn't ask too many questions.

"No, you're perfectly safe, Peyton."

"No! You don't understand, Ben. I didn't just crash my car because I was driving recklessly. I was trying to escape a dangerous situation. Someone was following me, and I ..."

Ben looked down. Was he trying to avoid my eyes? Was it too late? Was he ready to leave me? Great! Let's dump the crazy woman.

"Peyton, I have to tell you something."

Oh, no. Not the 'it's not you, it's me' speech. Not now! Not when Mateo was out there ready to pounce.

Oh, please, God. I can't lose Ben.

"It was me, Peyton." What was he talking about?

"I don't understand. What do you mean? What was you?"

"I was the one following you. I'm so fucking sorry."

"What?"

"I'm so sorry. I didn't mean for this to happen. I just wanted to see where you were going."

I stared at Ben without speaking, trying to figure out if I was happy that it wasn't Mateo chasing after me, or absolutely furious because Ben had been spying on me for no good reason.

"Please, Peyton, you have to believe me. I never would have followed you had I known it would scare you into racing off like that."

"You? But, why, Ben?"

"I care so much for you. Surely, you must know that by now. But I get the feeling that you're guarded when you're around me. I want to know everything about you, but I didn't want to push you. I realize you've been through hell, losing your baby, and leaving the man who was abusing you, but I want more, Peyton."

"So, you scared the living shit out of me, instead of just being patient?!"

"I'm so sorry."

I looked away and stared at the wall. Ben's eyes were so tender and his voice so remorseful. Was he really that insecure about me? I hadn't shut him out because I didn't care. I did it because I wanted to protect him.

And yourself, Peyton. You are afraid he'll leave you if he knows what a mess you've made of your life. Be honest with yourself for once!

"I'm sorry, Ben."

He looked at me with confusion on his face. As if he didn't hear me correctly.

"Sorry? No, Peyton. I'm sorry. It was a stupid thing to do."

"Yes, it was, but if I'm honest with myself I have to take some of the blame. You're right, Ben. I've been holding back. I knew you'd eventually want more, and I didn't think I was ready to give you that—to trust you—but I was wrong."

"You can, you know. Trust me. I'll never hurt you. Not intentionally, anyway."

"Ben, there's something I have to tell you. I just hope that once you know the truth you'll stick around."

"Come on. That's crazy. Nothing you tell me can be terrible enough for me to not want to be with you."

"I hope you mean that."

"Of course, I do."

"Okay. I don't even know where to start."

"Take your time, Peyton. I'm not going anywhere."

I took a deep breath and started at the beginning.

"I met someone, who I thought was special, in Mexico after my best friend and I got our degrees. He seemed the perfect guy—charming, sweet, thoughtful—I'm sure you can see where I'm going with this. Anyway, he asked me to marry him, and I said yes."

I took a quick break so I could have a sip of water. My mouth felt as if a rat had died in it. Bloody vomit. Ben sat perfectly still and waited for me to continue my tale of woe.

"At first, it was magical. He did everything right."

"Like me," Ben said softly.

I knew what he was thinking. I hoped that he was starting to understand why I'd been a little distant and held back. But I carried on talking.

"Then, once we began to settle into our happily ever after, was when he started to show his true colors. I was screwed. I'd ignored the initial warning sign, however faint, and went along and married a stranger. It was my own fault for being so gullible. I'm ashamed to admit that my pride kept me from dumping his ass right there and then."

I looked at Ben, who was listening intently to me. His eyes were filled with compassion for me. Had he put two and two together yet and figured out that he was sleeping with a married woman?

"So, I tried to make it work. It was a nightmare. Mateo was sullen, and mean, and seemed to enjoy torturing me. And what does a good wife do when that happens? I'll tell you what. She tries harder. Isn't that just fucking pathetic?"

"No, it isn't. It's part of the beautiful nature of a woman. You did what you thought you had to. Don't beat yourself up, Peyton."

I laughed out loud at the word 'beat', which wasn't the smartest move, as my head felt like it would split in half and my ribs ached like crazy. Ben must have thought I was losing my mind.

"No need to beat myself up. Mateo did that on a regular basis."

"Oh, Peyton. I'm so sorry," he said and cupped my face with his hand. "Son of a bitch. Forgive me for asking a stupid question, but why didn't you try and leave sooner?"

"I couldn't. He threatened to kill me or hurt my folks if I ever tried. So, I stayed."

Ben's face turned pink. I could tell that he was trying to keep his rage in check.

"Go on."

"This is where the story takes an ugly turn. Up until this point, I was Mateo's occasional punching bag, but things quickly spiraled out of control. I fell pregnant."

I swallowed at the memory of losing my baby, but I refused to give Mateo any more of my tears.

"Mateo was furious. He told me to get rid of our child, but I refused. I dug in my heels and went to see the gynecologist. If I thought my life was bad before, I soon learned that my nightmare had only just started."

"I don't understand. There was nothing wrong with your baby," Ben said.

"No, but there was something very wrong with its father. The gynecologist told me something that my husband had neglected to mention. You see, Mateo had been married before. Not once, but twice. Apparently, I was wife number three."

"You're kidding! Why wouldn't he say anything?"

"Oh, don't worry, it will make perfect sense very soon. Mateo kept it a secret from me because his previous two wives were missing."

"What? What do you mean?"

"I mean, they had vanished off the face of the earth."

"What did he say about that?"

"It wasn't what he said, but what he did when I confronted him with the truth."

"He threw you down the stairs," Ben said in a monotone.

"Bingo. He came home drunk, and I was stupid enough to take him on. I could have handled it better, in hindsight, but I was so mad I couldn't help myself. So, Mateo threw me down the basement stairs and killed my child."

"Fucking monster! I'm so sorry, Peyton. What a nightmare."

"It wasn't over."

I stopped talking and looked away. I was about to tell Ben the whole truth and I wasn't sure I was making the right decision.

"Please, go on, Peyton. You can trust me."

Ben took my hands and held them between his. His skin was warm, and the gesture tucked at my heart. Could I trust this man with the whole truth? I cared for him and the thought of not being able to be my true self with him was a bridge too far.

"I found something in the basement that scared me into action. I knew that I would have to get away from Mateo or I would die."

"What was it?"

"I found the missing women."

It looked like someone had slapped Ben in the face because he flinched at that revelation.

"Mateo murdered his wives, Ben. I found their dismembered bodies in freezers in the basement."

"Oh, God!"

"That was when I escaped. It wasn't easy, but I did it. Tonight, when you were chasing after me, I was sure I was about to die. I was convinced that Mateo had found me. I thought the gig was up, Ben."

"Fuck," he whispered. "I can't believe it. I'm truly sorry, Peyton. I wish you had told me sooner."

"How could I? It's bad enough that I have no faith left in men, but how could I know that you wouldn't run for the hills when you found out that I'm still married? I was too ashamed to tell you, Ben. And I'm terrified that Mateo will hurt you."

"Listen to me, Peyton," Ben said and wiped away the tears from my face. "Mateo will never hurt you again. Never! I won't allow it. You're safe with me. Now that I know the truth, I will protect you with my life. And I don't care that you are still married to him. We'll fix that."

"Mateo will never divorce me."

"We'll go to the police and have his monstrous ass thrown into prison."

"Mateo has the Mexican authorities in his pocket. It's no use. Promise me that you'll stay away from him, Ben. Swear it!"

"Okay, Peyton. I'll stay away from him. But you won't need to worry about him anymore. Move in with me. I'm in love with you, and I want you to live with me."

"Are you sure? I'm a mess, Ben, and you don't deserve to invite such chaos into your life. You're too good for that."

"Bull! I love you, Peyton. Take a chance on me. I swear to you, I won't let you down."

How could I refuse him? His eyes were warm and his voice thick with heartfelt sincerity.

"Please, Peyton."

"Okay. I'll move in with you. Thank you, Ben."

"You're safe with me, Peyton. I won't allow anything or anyone to hurt you again. Do you believe me?"

"I do. I love you too, Ben."

17

PEYTON

Moving into Ben's house was a challenge with one broken arm. Not that I had a mountain of earthly goods to move. Ben chuckled when I arrived at his place with two boxes.

"I had no idea you were a minimalist, Dr. Taylor," he teased.

"There's a lot about me you don't know, Dr. Forbes."

"I know you have the cutest heart-shaped birthmark on your left butt cheek. What else could I possibly need to know?"

"Spoken like a man who is looking to get him some," I grinned.

"Oh, yeah."

Ben picked me up and carried me to the bedroom.

"I think we'll start here," he said in a husky voice, "and then work our way through the entire house."

"In one day?"

"Hey, I'm good if you are."

"You're just showing off now, aren't you?" I chuckled.

"Are you impressed?" he purred.

"Seriously."

Ben kissed me slowly, passionately.

"I love you, Peyton," he whispered into my ear and traced his tongue along the lobe.

I had goosebumps all over, and my nipples were hard as granite in anticipation of his touch.

"I want you naked," he moaned and started to undress me.

I was dizzy with desire as he removed my clothes. Every touch of his hands sent a thrilling sensation into my core. Ben was gentle, careful not to hurt my arm or my ribs, which were still bruised from the impact.

My lover removed his clothes while I lay on my back on the bed, watching every move that he made.

"You are so sexy, Ben," I smiled.

"You ain't seen nothing yet, my dear," he said with a smirk and pulled me gently to the foot of the bed, so my bottom was close to the edge.

My desire kicked up a good few notches at the thought of what he was about to do to me. The hair on my neck stood up as Ben kneeled at the foot of the bed.

I closed my eyes in anticipation. My lover guided my ankles onto the bed, positioning me perfectly so that he would have easy access to my wet, swollen core. For the first time since we'd first made love, I surrendered not only my body but also my soul to the man who had so patiently opened up my heart again to love.

With his tongue, Ben tasted and teased me, and when I thought I couldn't possibly be any more aroused, he took me higher. My body quivered as he sucked, licked, and played.

"Tell me you want me," he whispered when I thought I couldn't take anymore.

"I want you, Ben," I offered without an ounce of doubt.

That was when he lay on top of me and drove excitedly into me. The sensation brought me immediately to an explosive orgasm. I moaned and gasped excitedly as I rode the waves of ecstasy. On and on went my climax. Unending, heavy with pleasure.

Ben moved inside of me, faster, harder, until his orgasm exploded into my being.

"I love you, Peyton," he said again, his breath still racing with excitement.

"I love you, Ben."

This time, I truly understood what the words meant. I was truly in love.

* * *

"My family is excited about meeting you," Ben said one afternoon. "I thought we could have them over for lunch on Sunday. Would you be okay with that?"

"Hhm, meeting the parents. What if they don't like me?" I asked, genuinely nervous.

"Well, in that case, I'll miss them terribly," he laughed.

"Come on, Ben. I'm serious."

"My love, how can someone so incredible be so insecure? My family will love you, as I do."

"It's not insecurity, Ben. I don't know if they will want me around you when they find out about my past. And I wouldn't blame them either."

"Then, let's not tell them. Okay?"

"And lie?"

"It's not lying. There's no sense in telling my family and worrying them unnecessarily."

"Thank you, my love," I said and pulled Ben in for a long embrace.

Living with him was amazing. He brought me coffee every morning and shared the cooking duties with me. Ben never drank too much, and he *never* had an unkind word for me. I was honestly the happiest I'd ever been.

"Okay, so I'll tell them this Sunday. We'll have a barbecue."

"Great. I'll make a cheesecake."

"And, just like that you're the perfect woman."

* * *

I felt a little silly after I'd been so nervous about meeting Ben's family. He was right. His family was as kind and easygoing as he was.

"Mom, Dad, this is Payton. Darling, meet Alan and Frances Forbes."

"Hello, Peyton," Alan said and kissed me on the cheek. "Lovely to meet you."

"Oh, my goodness," Frances added, "you are even more beautiful than Ben said. It's lovely to meet you, Peyton."

"Is Owen coming, sweetheart?" Frances asked Ben.

"Yeah, he and Suzy will be along soon."

I was looking forward to meeting Ben's brother. Ben spoke so fondly of him that I just knew I would love him.

"So, Peyton. Ben tells us you're a doctor too. Have you decided which field you're going to pursue?" Alan asked me.

"I'm still weighing up my options," I said, as I honestly hadn't decided yet.

"Ben says you're very smart," Frances added.

"Oh, he's very sweet," I smiled and blushed.

"It's true. You are a brilliant intern. You can do anything you set your mind to," Ben cooed, making me love him just a little more right then.

"Thank you."

The front door opened and in stepped a very handsome man accompanied by a woman with black hair and a beautiful smile. Owen looked so much like Ben. Except his eyes were different.

"Hey, little brother. Come on in. Hi, Suzy. Good to see you," Ben said and embraced the newcomers.

"Hi, I'm Suzy," the lovely woman greeted me with a smile. "So nice to meet you, Peyton."

"Hi, Suzy. It's a pleasure."

"Ahh, the lovely Peyton," Owen said, and kissed me on the cheek, before he turned to Ben and said, "I don't know what you're on about, Ben. She's not that ugly."

Everyone started laughing. The ice was broken. Ben slapped his brother on the shoulder and rolled his eyes.

"Sorry, Peyton. I told you my brother wasn't altogether house-trained yet."

The afternoon went by so quickly. Ben's family was a delight, and it was truly heartwarming to watch the two boys ribbing one another. Suzy offered to help me fetch the cheesecake and plates from the kitchen.

"Wow. Ben is crazy about you," she said once we were out of earshot.

"That's good because I feel the same way about him."

"He's such a lovely guy. You got yourself a good one, Peyton," she smiled.

"Owen seems like a barrel of laughs."

"And then some. Honestly, he keeps me sane. My mother is a serious pain in the backside. If it weren't for Owen, I think I would have been a feature on the Crime Channel a long time ago."

I couldn't help laughing.

"Sorry, that was insensitive of me," I offered.

"That's all right. I'd laugh too if it wasn't such a nightmare," she said and winked.

"Yeah, family can be a curse," I said, trying not to go into too much detail.

"So you know," Suzy grinned.

"Oh, yeah. I know."

"Ben tells us you are new to New York. Are you coping with the pace?"

"It took a while, but I think I've got the measure of the place. Have you lived here long?"

"Born and bred. Have you been to a baseball game yet?"

"No, I haven't really had time yet. It's been crazy at the hospital. Being a resident isn't for the fainthearted."

"I suppose not."

"What do you do?"

"I'm in advertising. I have the pleasure of dealing with pedantic wannabe starlets. Then again, I suppose I've had excellent practice all my life. You know, Mom and all," she grinned.

"That sounds exciting."

"It can be."

"So, I take it you're a baseball fan?"

"Oh, hugely! We should go some time. You'll love it. I'll even stick you to a hotdog with all the fixings."

"You had me at hotdog," I smiled.

Ben's folks left at about 8 pm.

"Ugh! I ate way too much," I said and rubbed my stomach.

"Your cheesecake was a hit. Almost as much as you."

"Ahhh, thank you, Ben. Your family is lovely. I don't know why I was nervous."

"I told you. What did you think of Suzy?"

"She's very nice. She invited me to watch a baseball game with her."

"Yeah, Suzy knows her stuff when it comes to baseball."

"I'm looking forward to it. Thank you, babe."

"For what?"

"For believing in me. In us."

"Are you kidding? I just didn't want you to sue me for hospital expenses after your accident," he smirked.

"Funny guy," I said and play-punched him on the arm.

Ben grabbed the arm and held it behind my back.

"Watch it, missy," he purred, "you only have one at the moment. Imagine what I can do to you if I hold onto it," he teased and nibbled on my nipple through my shirt.

"That reminds me," I laughed, "you need to teach me some more karate moves, Buster."

"Of course. But first I'm going to show you a few of my gynecologist moves," he said, picked me up, carried me to the bedroom, and rocked my world.

* * *

"Hi, Mom, it's me."

"Peyton, my love. What's wrong? Are you alright?"

My poor parents were on a knife's edge since I'd shared the truth about Mateo with them. I felt so awful about that.

"I'm alright, Mom. Nothing's wrong. Just calling to say hi."

"Oh, goodness. My heart skipped a beat there. So nice of you to call, my love. How are you?"

"I'm so well, Mom. I moved in with Ben."

I didn't tell them about the accident. I'd put my parents through enough.

"I see."

"Don't worry, Mom," I said when I heard her hesitant tone. "He's nothing like Mateo. Ben is lovely and he's very protective over me."

"In that case, I'm happy for you, Peyton."

"Thank you, Mom. How are you guys doing? Madi must be popping out of her clothes."

"Yes, the poor dear is taking a bit of strain this time around. She's so busy with the boys too. I wish she'd use me more. But you know Madison. She's a DIY girl when it comes to her family."

"That she is."

"How are you really, Pey? I'm sorry. Here I am banging on about Madison's pregnancy."

"Don't be silly, Mom. I'm very happy for her. Please, don't worry about me. I'm doing well. I really am. Being with Ben has made all the difference. I don't know what I would have done if it weren't for him."

"When can we meet him?"

"I'll have to give that one some thought. But I'll find a way of getting you all together safely."

"I hate that you have to hide like this, my love. It isn't right."

"I hate it too, but I know Mateo. He'll be watching you. I'm so thankful that I managed to sneak in and out of town to see you the last time. I find that I'm still holding my breath without realizing it every time I leave the house or the hospital. It's such a burden."

"He won't find you, baby. You're being so careful. And don't worry about us. We understand your predicament. It's just that I miss you terribly."

"I miss you too, Mom."

I'd learned to treasure my telephone conversations with my family. Madison and I spoke often, and I called home to talk to Mom and Dad at least once a week. I was sure I couldn't be traced as I always used a burner phone.

Just in case.

18

BEN

"I have a surprise for you, sexy," I told Peyton one morning early when I delivered her usual morning cuppa.

"Hhmm, coffee," she said in a sleepy tone.

"Okay. I have two surprises for you."

Peyton opened her eyes and rolled onto her back.

"Good morning, handsome," she smiled and stretched out lazily.

"Hello, beautiful. Did you sleep well?"

"Like a log, thanks. What's this about a surprise?"

"I'm taking you away for the weekend."

"What about work?"

"All taken care of."

"Ooh, that sounds like fun. Where are we going?"

"That's the surprise part."

"You're not going to make me fish again, are you?"

"What? Do you mean to tell me you aren't a fishing convert? And after I spent all that time cleaning your catch. How rude," I teased and bent down to kiss her beautiful lips.

"Hey, I'm happy that you have your passions. But I'm happy to send you off with a picnic basket and some beer."

"Oh, well. Can't blame a guy for trying. Anyway, no, it's not a fishing trip."

"In that case...yay!" she said, yawned, and grinned.

"It's a good thing you're so cute. Otherwise, I'd dump your fishing-hating butt right now," I said and climbed into bed with her.

"I do have other qualities you may find enjoyable," she purred and reached into my shorts.

"Oh, who cares about fish, anyway?" I smiled and proceeded to ravage my gorgeous lover.

Making love to Peyton was an experience I'd always treasure. Since she shared her past with me, our intimacy had taken on a whole new dimension. She's given herself to me fully, and that made all the difference. It wasn't that sex was bad before, on the contrary. But there was a tenderness and a vulnerability now that was spellbinding. I was deeply and completely in love with her.

Peyton's arm was healed, and she no longer flinched when she laughed, so I assumed that the bruising around her ribs had also subsided. Unfortunately, her psyche was still a little spooked.

I noticed small things that she did when she didn't know I was watching. For instance, she would check the rearview mirror way too often while we drove somewhere. Sure, New York was a crazy place to drive, but even so, I knew she was looking for Mateo.

Also, she chewed her lip whenever we left the house or the hospital. I couldn't imagine what she must have been going through, but I thought I'd give her a break for a few days and take her away to a mountain retreat where it would be just the two of us.

"Do you ski?" I asked her after we'd made love.

"Water, ice, or snow?"

"Snow."

"A little. I'm not exactly James Bond, but I get by. Why?"

"Because, my delectable sexpot, I've booked us into a mountain lodge where all we'll be doing is skiing, drinking red wine, and bonking like rabbits on a fur rug in front of a fireplace for three whole days and nights. What do you think about that?"

"I think you're the perfect man," Peyton said excitedly. "When do we go?"

"How quickly can you pack?"

"Pack? What for? Sounds like we're going to be naked most of the time. Who needs clothes?"

"Now who's perfect?" I laughed and nuzzled her neck.

* * *

"Oh, Ben. It's perfect!" Peyton exclaimed when we entered the private cabin I'd secured for the long weekend.

The cabin was more modern than I'd expected, but it retained the feel of one hidden away in the woods. I was pretty pleased with myself, especially when I saw the joy and excitement in Peyton's eyes.

"There's a shop nearby that rents out ski equipment. Shall we unpack and get you kitted up?" I asked.

"Sounds good."

The shop assistant was very helpful and soon Peyton and I were off to do a bit of skiing.

"Okay," she said, looking every bit the professional in her new gear, "here goes nothing."

Peyton pushed the poles into the ground and off she went.

"You fibber! Looks to me like you've been skiing all your life," I laughed as she sped past me down the hill.

"Loser has to do the cleaning up after dinner," she shouted back.

I clipped into my skis and raced after the little sneak. It took some fancy footwork to catch up to her. Peyton had turned out to be more and more interesting the better I got to know her.

She was laughing hysterically once I caught up to her. Mission accomplished! Peyton was free.

"That was amazing," she said, catching her breath.

"I'm so happy you enjoyed it, my love."

My cherub's cheeks were flushed, and her eyes danced as she smiled at me. Job done!

"Come on, let's get back to the cabin," I said after an hour and a half.

"Great idea. I could do with a glass of red and a bite to eat. I've forgotten how hungry I get while I'm showing off on the snow."

"I certainly won't forget this. It's twice you've surprised me now. First the fishing and now this. What else are you an expert in?"

"Light that fire and I'll show you," she said with an impish grin.

"Where's that ski lift?" I said and clicked off my skis.

Peyton laughed and did the same. The lift took us back up the mountain to the base of the ski resort, and we did the ten-minute drive back to the cabin from there.

"It's so calm and peaceful here, Ben. I can hear myself thinking up here. New York is very exciting, but how lovely it must be to live here in the mountains. Imagine, I'd grow herbs in pots on the windowsill and you'd hunt for deer. Couldn't you just picture it?"

"You make it sound so doable, Pey."

"Why couldn't it be?"

"Well, for a start, I'd have to walk away from a very lucrative business."

"There's no reason you couldn't establish your practice here. You'd make a fine family gynie. All the local bored, rich housewives would flock to the pretty new doctor."

"Are you pimping me out?"

"Absolutely."

"And what about your residency Dr. Taylor?"

"I'd find a local hospital and finish it here. I've always wanted to live in a small town where I'm the country doctor. I'd be the local Dr. Quinn, Medicine Woman," she grinned. "Except, instead of raking in the cash, I'd barter my services for ducks, chickens, and deer."

"And our kids? Will we let them run wild in the mountains and collect berries for pies?" I asked.

Peyton's expression changed. She was less jovial suddenly.

Ben, you idiot!

"I'm sorry, my love. I wasn't thinking," I said and took her hand.

She smiled at me, but I could see my comment about children had rattled her.

"It's okay. It doesn't hurt so much anymore."

She was lying to make me feel less guilty to spare my feelings—as if she was trying to protect me. I felt like an elephant stomping clumsily through a rose garden.

We shared a warm bath when we got back to the cabin. I opened a bottle of red wine and threw on a few steaks while Peyton dried her hair.

"You look snug," I said when she emerged from the bedroom.

"Hmm, it smells good in here."

"I opened the bottle. Would you mind pouring us a glass?"

"Sure."

"Do you want some kale with your steak?" I asked when she handed me a glass of Merlot.

"Hell, no. I hate kale," she said and pulled a face.

"Ooh, a true carnivore."

"Yup, cut off the horns, wipe the rear, and scare it in the pan. That's how I like it."

"I remember. You would have been a very desirable cavewoman," I laughed.

Peyton's mood was back to its playful self. The way it was before I fucked it up. I was grateful.

We sat down to a lovely meal and then retired at the fire. The glow of the flames lit up her beautiful face.

"I was thinking about what you said," I commented while we sat together, staring into the amber tongues.

"Which part?" she asked.

"The part about leaving the chaos of the city behind and moving to a place like this."

"Oh?"

"Uh-huh. It may not be such a crazy idea."

"Really?"

"Yeah. We could make it work. Why not?"

"Imagine," she said, staring into the fire.

"It's a dream worth pursuing."

Oh, I'm just being silly, I guess," she said after a long pause. "It's too perfect."

"I know what you're thinking, Peyton. You can talk to me, you know."

"The truth is, Ben, I don't know if I'll ever be truly content anywhere. You deserve to know that. I don't know if I can live with the guilt of depriving you of a happy, relaxed life."

"You're talking about Mateo, aren't you?"

"Yes. He's never going to give me up. I know too much."

"What if he wasn't an issue anymore?" I asked.

"What do you mean?"

"What if Mateo goes away forever?"

"I don't like the way this conversation is going, Ben. You promised me you wouldn't do anything foolish."

"I'm not saying I will. I'm merely suggesting that it's a possibility."

Peyt0n started nibbling on her lower lip. She didn't say anything, but I knew she was stressing about me.

I turned to her and took her gently by the shoulders so she could face me.

151

"Mateo isn't the only one with connections, babe. I have access to military men who will do whatever I ask of them, given the situation."

"I couldn't carry on if anything happened to you, Ben. The loss will be too great."

"Nothing is going to happen to me. I promise. Please, allow me to make a few calls. Just calls. No heroics."

Peyton's eyes teared up. I wiped away the wet trail a wayward tear had left behind when it spilled down her cheek.

"Okay," she whispered.

"Okay," I echoed and held her close to my chest. "I want to give you your dream, Peyton. I want you to realize all the dreams you've ever had. They are beautiful dreams."

Peyton threw her arms around my neck and sobbed. I recognized the need for release, so I simply held onto her until she stopped.

Afterward, I made love to my precious Peyton in front of the log fire. It was beautiful because it was raw with emotion. I vowed to myself then that I would do anything and everything in my power to ensure that she never had to shed another tear of regret again.

The weekend flew by, as do all things that feel as if they are too good to be true. Peyton and I drove back to the city on Monday and by Tuesday we were back at the salt mines. My patient list was full, so I didn't see much of my love for a good few days. Catching babies and looking after women's reproductive health kept me on my toes.

But, all the while, I kept one person in my thoughts. Mateo Garcia. I was going to get to that fucking murdering psychopath if it was the last thing I ever did. Even if I had to fly to Mexico and do it myself.

Fortunately, it would come to that. I had plenty of connections who would be more than happy to root out a piece of shit like Mateo. The man was a skid mark on the underpants of society. I could think of nothing more deplorable than a man like him, and I would not rest until he was either someone's bitch in prison, where he belonged, or six feet under.

Enjoy your freedom, Mateo. It won't last long. I'm coming for you and I'm going to rain down hell's fury upon your murderous head.

19

PEYTON

"I have a week off and I'd love to see you, Pey," Alyssa said one morning while we were chatting on the phone. "It bugs me that I know nothing about where you live or what Ben is like. Can't I come and visit you?"

"Lyssa. You know how I feel about that. What if Mateo is watching?"

"Come on, Pey. It's been months now and we've seen neither hide nor hair of him. I'll be careful, I promise. I'll even dress as a weirdo so he, or whomever you think is watching me, won't recognize me. P.l.e.e.e.a.s.e."

I couldn't help giggling at her silly voice. I supposed she had a point. It had been almost six months since I escaped his claws, and no one had seen or heard from him. Plus, I really missed my friend.

"Okay."

"Great!"

"But, please, I know I sound like a broken record, Lyss, be careful."

"Of course."

"I'll ask Ben to collect you from the airport. That way I don't have to send you, my address. It's better for both of us if you don't have anything like that on your phone or pc."

"Or we could do it Mission Impossible style with a self-destructing note," she said in a put-on accent.

"Uh-huh. And to which mountain range do I send the communication?"

Alyssa laughed.

"Okay, never mind. I'm not a fan of heights."

"When will you come?"

"The end of next week, if that isn't too soon."

"No, that will work. Speaking of which, I will have to work a few shifts while you're here."

"No problem. I'll keep myself occupied."

"Cool."

So, it was official. Alyssa was going to meet Ben. It was exciting, actually. She'd be the first person from my close-knit group to do so. I wasn't concerned that she wouldn't like Ben. Who wouldn't like him? The man was near perfect.

I discussed it with him the next morning.

"Babe, Alyssa wants to come for a visit. I told her it's okay."

"Oh, nice. It will be lovely meeting your best friend. When is she coming?"

"The end of next week."

"I'm looking forward to it."

"Would you do me a favor and collect her from the airport, please, Ben?"

"Absolutely."

"Thank you," I said and hugged him.

"Careful, I have to go to work now. If you keep pressing that irresistible body up against me, someone else will have to catch the babies today," he said in a husky voice.

"Why, Dr. Forbes," I giggled, "what would the board say?"

"Not a damn thing if they could see you naked," he chuckled and kissed me passionately.

"You'd better let me go then, my love."

"Ugh! Okay, but we're finishing this later."

"Yes, Sir."

"Ooh, I like that," he said and patted my butt.

I was excited about Alyssa's visit. There was just something about being with someone who'd known you for almost a lifetime that resonated. Alyssa and I had been through all the milestones together, and she knew me better than anyone. She even kept the little notes and letters I wrote her when we were teenagers.

She brought out a box once and hauled out a stack of letters. We laughed so much while reading them. I couldn't believe I was such a nut back then. How time and circumstances changed one's outlook on life. What I wouldn't have given to turn back the clock to a time when my biggest concern was what to wear to Macy's birthday party.

The weeks flew by in a haze and before I knew it, it was Friday and Ben was off to collect Alyssa from the airport. I wondered what the two of them would talk about on the way home. I imagined that my best friend would ever so subtly interrogate Ben, and I wondered if he'd pick up on that.

I went downstairs when I heard Ben's car pull up.

"Honey, I'm home," Alyssa's voice echoed from the entrance hall.

"Hey!" I called and grabbed her in a bear hug.

"Ooh," she said and held on tightly, "it's sooo good to see you!"

We stood there for a good minute.

"He's amazing," she whispered into my ear.

"I know," I whispered back.

"Okay, kids," Ben said when he'd placed Alyssa's bag on the floor. "I have to get back to work. No parties and don't burn the place down while I go back to work to bring home the bacon," he grinned.

"Thanks, babe," I said and kissed him before he left.

"Sure thing, gorgeous. I'll see you later."

"See you."

I'd arranged to have the day off, so Alyssa and I could spend it together. There was so much to catch up on.

"I brought you a little something," she announced while she was unpacking. "Here."

She handed me an envelope.

"What's this?"

"Open it."

Inside, were pieces of paper that were folded over. I unfurled one and saw that it was a letter. I read it quietly while Alyssa carried on unpacking.

Dear Peyton,
I'm so jealous that Lyssa gets to spend the week with you. I wish it were me. I miss you, Sis.

The baby is growing like a weed. It seems every day I gain another butt cheek. The boys are getting impatient. They keep asking if I'm sure the baby is a girl. I showed them the picture of the scan and now they're convinced their new sibling is an alien. Poor Jamie was completely grossed out when I explained to him where his sister will 'hatch' from. I tell you, having three small kids is going to be tricky. I wish you were here to share in my madness. I think of you often, Pey. I can't believe you went through so much on your own. You're so brave, Sis. I hope we'll get to spend more time together soon. Once the baby comes it will be all hands on deck on this side. I try to sneak in a quick power nap in the afternoon when the boys have theirs, but what are the odds of all three kids sleeping at the same time once Gabbi is born? Oh, yeah, we've decided to name her Gabriella.

Anyway, I'm happy that Alyssa will be with you for a bit. I hope you'll visit us again soon. I love you, Peyton. I'm here if you need to talk.

Hugs and kisses

Madison

"No! Stop bubbling, you," Alyssa said when she saw my tears. "This was supposed to make you happy, not sad."

"Ugh! I can't help myself. This is so thoughtful, Lyssa."

"I can't take the credit, I'm afraid. When I told your family about my visit, they insisted on sending you a note each. Your family loves you very much, Pey."

"You know, Lyssa. It's crazy how we take family and friends for granted until they're thousands of miles away. I'm so glad you bugged me to visit. I've been so afraid of getting anyone hurt, but I see now that I was really hurting myself more."

"Uh-huh. That's the truth. Why should you cut out the people who love you because you're afraid of one man?"

"He's not exactly your average menace, Lyssa."

"I understand that, and I don't for a minute diminish the threat he poses to all of us, but you aren't alone anymore. We are all here for you and we'll protect you."

"I love you, Lyssa."

"Okay, enough of that," she said and hauled out a brown paper bag. "Let's kick this reunion into high gear!"

Alyssa whipped out a bottle of tequila and three lemons.

"Point me to the salt and shot glasses, please, doctor!"

"Come along, you nut. Follow me."

The two of us spent the afternoon giggling like teenagers as we recounted our miss spent teenage years. We were well on our way to being drunk by the time Ben joined us after work.

"I see you ladies had a good day," he smiled when I hugged and kissed him.

"Yup!"

"Hungry, girls?"

"Starving," Alyssa answered.

"I'll throw a few steaks on the grill," he winked.

"I don't suppose you have other cuties like you waiting in the wings, do you, Ben?" Alyssa grinned.

"Nope," I cooed. "They broke the mold after my Adonis."

"I better grill that meat, STAT," Ben laughed.

* * *

"So...what did you and Alyssa talk about yesterday on the way home from the airport?" I asked Ben when we woke up the next morning.

"I can't reveal my intel," he chuckled and nibbled on my nipple.

"Don't you try and distract me, you sneak," I giggled, and slapped his bare ass.

Ben covered my mouth with his and kissed me, long and slow. What the hell. It was pointless engaging my brain when he did that. All I could focus on was getting him inside of me so I could ride the magical wave of orgasm to its shuddering conclusion.

Ben's magic fingers explored my body and soon we were moving together in a frenzied bout of delicious grinding. I threw back my head when I exploded in an earth-shattering climax. Ben followed almost instantly.

I laid my head on his wet chest as we tried to catch our breath.

"You certainly know your way around the clitoris, Doc," I heaved.

"Well, I am a skilled gynecologist, you know. I have years of intense scrutiny and science behind me," he chuckled.

"Have you had many lovers?"

"Why? Are you jealous?"

"Extremely," I said and bit down gently on his nipple.

Ben jerked.

"Ooph! Didn't see that one coming, you naughty girl."

"What do you think of Alyssa?" I asked again.

"She's lovely. I can see why you and she are so close. She's a genuine human being. I'm sure I don't have to tell you how much she loves you. She made it crystal clear that she'd rip out my spine if I did anything to hurt you. And I believed her."

I laughed at the thought of Alyssa holding a finger in Ben's face, threatening him. She would have been more subtle, obviously, but I imagined her message came through loud and clear.

"I think her protective nature has kicked up a notch or two since the Mateo disaster. My whole family has been on high alert, I'm afraid. She means well."

"Don't misunderstand me. I didn't mind her candor at all. It makes me like her more, actually. At least I know whose side she's on."

It was Saturday, so Ben didn't have to go to work. I, on the other hand, had to show my face at the hospital or they'd kick me into touch.

"I wish I didn't have to work today," I moaned when I reluctantly dragged myself out of bed.

"I know. I'm going to miss you. Don't worry about Alyssa. I'll take her on a tour of the city, you know, touristy stuff."

"You don't mind, babe?"

"Hey, I think it's a good way of staying on her good side," he smirked. "I need all the points I can gather."

"You have more points than you'll ever need, but that's a very kind gesture. Thanks, my love."

"You're welcome."

I had a quick shower, got dressed, and left for work, leaving Alyssa behind to sleep in, and Ben to catch up on some reports. It was a good day. No one died.

Alyssa's visit flew by in the blink of an eye. I cried my eyes out when Ben took her back to the airport. He was extra sweet to me once she'd gone—he taught me a few extra karate 101 moves to distract me.

Not that my training got me to an expert level. Not with all the sex it seemed to initiate whenever he got me on my back in the dojo. But, hey, I wasn't complaining.

My life was perfect. Well, almost.

20

BEN

Peyton was on a high. The week she'd spent with Alyssa had done her the world of good. I tried my best to distract her once her best friend had left, but, honestly, I knew there was only way the love of my life would ever be truly happy. I had to do something about Mateo. He needed to disappear from the picture. Altogether.

But, how? How would I manage the Herculean task of bringing Mateo to justice in a place where he seemed to be protected from all sides?

Peyton and I had spoken about it when we were away at the ski weekend, but I hadn't done anything about it. I realized after Alyssa had been and gone that the time to make good on my promises was at hand, so I called a friend of mine who served alongside me in the armed forces.

"Doc! How are you?" Sam greeted me when he answered my call.

"Hey, Sam. All good. How're they hanging?"

It was a little joke we shared. Sam very nearly lost his left testicle one night in an enemy attack when a bullet grazed his nether regions.

Thankfully, I was on call and able to prevent him from having to suffer involuntary neutering.

"Swinging happily, thanks, Doc. To what do I owe the pleasure, Ben?"

"Are you free for a drink sometime this week? I have a little undercover project for you."

"Sounds intriguing. I'm in. How about tomorrow night?"

"Great. I'll send you a pin location."

"Good to hear from you, Ben. I'll see you tomorrow."

"Thanks, Sam."

Peyton was on the night shift that whole week, so I didn't have to be concerned about leaving her alone at the house. I never told her, but it made me nervous when she was there by herself. I even contemplated buying a large dog to protect her, but we were both too busy with our careers to care for a puppy. So, instead, I had a kickass security system installed.

I met Sam the following evening at 6 pm for a drink and a chat.

"You look good, Ben. Still tickling titties and caressing clitorises?" he chuckled.

"Yup. Still beating the snot out of transgressors, and keeping an eye on wandering spouses?"

"Ouch! Good one. Yes, I'm still the answer to all matters clandestine and otherwise. I must say, you look like a man who doesn't have one stuck in the chamber. Who is she?"

"That obvious, is it?"

"Yup."

"I take then that this isn't a social call."

"I'm afraid not. Sam, I've got a really big problem and I need your help."

"Sounds serious, Ben. Are you in danger?" Sam asked with a look of genuine concern.

"Not me, specifically, but my girlfriend could use some help."

"Okay. I'm listening."

I told Sam the whole sordid tale, after which he told me he would look into it on my behalf.

"This guy sounds like a real scumbag. It isn't going to be easy getting the measure of him all the way in Mexico. But I have a few trusted connections I can talk to."

"Great. As I said, please, be careful who you talk to over there. This guy has the local authorities in his back pocket, so asking the wrong man for help could end up in an ugly mess."

"I hear you, Ben. Don't worry about that. As I said, I know some quality people in Mexico City. I'll need a few days to get the ball rolling, but it shouldn't take too long."

"Thanks, Sam. I appreciate it."

"Not at all, Doc. I owe you that much seeing as you managed to save my left nut."

I laughed at his grimace.

"You're too kind, Sam," I said and slapped him on the back of his shoulder.

"Tell me about your new lady."

"Peyton's a doctor too—a resident—smart as hell, and even sexier than she is intelligent."

"I must say, Ben. I haven't seen you quite this lyrical about a woman. She must be something."

"I'm crazy about her."

"It sounds like she's been through the wringer with this Mateo guy."

"Yeah. You'd drive over there and kill him with your bare hands if I told you all the despicable things, he'd done to her. He threw her down a flight of stairs while pregnant with their child. What kind of a monster does that to a woman?"

"One that needs to be removed from civilization, I'd say."

"Yeah."

"Let's see what I can dig up on him first. We'll tear him a new one later," Sam smiled.

"Deal."

"In the meantime, don't you get any Karate Kid ideas. You feeling me, buddy?"

"Uh-huh."

"I mean it, Ben. Leave this to me. I can't have you walk into a situation you can't escape from."

"I'll wait for you."

"You do that. Now, buy me a whiskey, and let's not talk shop anymore."

* * *

Sam called me back three days later. I'd been waiting to hear from him with trepidation, checking my phone for missed calls whenever I'd been away from the damn thing.

"Sam. Talk to me."

"Hey, Ben. Jeez, you weren't kidding about this guy. He's bad news on an epic scale."

"I told you he was no good."

"I've had someone keep an eye on him for a few days now. He has some interesting habits."

"I'm sure."

"He likes to smack the fairer sex around some. My contact followed him to a house of ill repute if you catch my drift, and let's just say he likes to leave his whores behind, battered and bruised."

"I can't believe this man was married to Peyton. The idea just blows my mind, Sam."

"Sociopaths are very charming when they want to be. That is what makes them so difficult to spot. He's a benevolent, successful, charming, and apparently pretty good-looking man, as far as most are concerned. But scratch the surface enough, and out pours a freak of nature."

"I need to stop him, Sam."

"No. You don't 'need' to do a thing about Mateo Garcia. You need to take care of Peyton. I'll keep an eye on the guy, until such time as we've thought of a fitting punishment."

"What did you have in mind?"

"That depends on you, I suppose."

"What do you mean?"

"If you want him dead, we'll do it. But someone like Mateo will be better served in prison where he can get a little payback for his abhorrent behavior. If you get my drift. Death is far too easy for this clown."

"I agree. He must rot in prison where the inmates can show him some TLC. Besides, what good am I as a person if I become a murderer myself? I couldn't look Peyton in the eye."

"My thoughts exactly."

"There's just one problem. There's no way his connections will sit back and fold their hands if he's arrested in Mexico. He's too valuable an asset to the cops. The man is rather generous with his Pesos when it comes to paying off the cops. He's the proverbial golden goose to them."

"How are we going to get around that?" I asked, irritated at this critical hurdle in my plans.

"Well, the only way we're going to make this stick is to have him arrested on American soil."

"But what about the extradition treaty? The government will simply send him back to Mexico."

"True. But at least then Mexico has to do something. It will be all over the news. What a juicy story for the press! Have you ever seen the media descending like flies on a turd when the words serial killer is mentioned? Mateo Garcia will be an international headline."

"Yeah, I suppose killing two wives and attempting to do the same to another will get the tongues wagging."

"And then some," Sam echoed. "I don't think you'll have to worry too much about Mateo Garcia after that. Also, the families of his previous wives will be out for blood too."

"Okay. Now, how do we get him here? He isn't likely to accept an invitation to pop over the border for a visit. How do we get him here?" I asked.

Sam was right. There would have to be a pretty big carrot dangling somewhere in the wings in the States to get Mateo to leave Mexico where his nest was comfortably feathered.

"There is one way that springs to mind," Sam started.

I knew exactly what he was going to say.

"Absolutely not! I will not use Peyton as bait. She's been through enough. Besides, she's so traumatized by that bastard I doubt whether she'd be able to do it even if I asked her to. So, no. Sorry, Sam. We'll have to think of another way."

"That makes my plan more difficult, Ben, but not impossible. Let me see if I can get my contacts to suggest a way. They're watching him anyway, so perhaps they are able to find out more about his habits. Perhaps he's planning on traveling somewhere soon. We'll nab him then."

"Thanks, Sam. I really appreciate this. I owe you large, my friend."

"Nonsense. You don't owe me a damn thing. Anything for a fellow soldier. You know that."

"Okay. Keep me posted, please, Sam. I need to know the minute Mateo even thinks of leaving Mexico."

"Don't you worry your delicate surgeon's hands, Ben. I've got my guy on him twenty-four-seven."

"I feel better already. Talk soon. Thanks, Sam."

"Sure thing."

I felt much better after having talked the situation through with Sam. I was still infuriated because I couldn't get to the monster who'd hurt my Peyton so badly, but at least we were one step closer to getting justice.

Peyton was doing well. Although, I knew she was missing her family. I half expected her to jump into Alyssa's bag and fly home with her. I wondered when the next trip would come. I was uneasy the first time she'd traveled to see her folks and sister. That was before I knew about Mateo.

I couldn't imagine how sick with worry I'd be the next time she decided to go. At least Sam's guy was surveilling Mateo, so even though he would always be in the back of my mind, at least he would be where we could keep an eye on him.

I called Peyton.

"Hey, gorgeous, woman."

"Well, hello Doctor Goldfingers. This is a nice surprise."

"How would you like to go out to dinner later?"

"That sounds lovely. Where were you thinking?"

"What are you in the mood for?"

"There's a new Chinese restaurant downtown. Olivia says they're the bomb."

"Chinese it is, my gorgeous."

"You're in a good mood."

"Indeed."

"What's the occasion?"

"Come now. Don't force me to get all cheesy on you."

"Try me. I'm sure I can take it."

"Okay, but you asked for it," I said and heard Peyton chuckling on the line. "There's no occasion, Pey. I just love you so much. Enough to feed you whatever your precious heart desires."

"Okay, hang on. I need to find a bucket," she teased.

"You see. I told you," I laughed.

"Yup. You certainly warned me."

She laughed out loud.

"I love you too, Ben. And later tonight, when I'm all hyped up on moo shu pork, I'll show you just how much."

"Yay! Sex!"

"Not just any sex, baby. Chinese food inspired, sweet and sticky sex."

"I think I'd better hang up now," I moaned. "My next patient is waiting, and I have a very bothersome hardon to contend with."

"Really? Wanna know what color my g-string is?"

"Stop that, you cheeky vixen."

"Red."

"I'm hanging up now."

"Coward," she giggled.

"Bye-bye, baby."

"Later sexy."

Hmm, what to do with a raging hardon? I had a few ideas, but my patient was waiting, so I thought of the unsexist thing I could imagine. I didn't have to think too hard.

The thought of Mateo Garcia took care of my growing problem.

21

PEYTON

Madison was due any day, and my heart was sore. I wanted to be with her. Was it because I was emotional over the fact that my baby also would have been due soon? Perhaps. Who truly knew the heart of a woman who has lost a child?

"What's wrong, my love?" Ben asked.

"Nothing. Why?"

"Come on. I know that look. Besides, you're nibbling on your lip again."

"Ugh. I hate that you've learned to know me so well," I said and rolled my eyes.

"Uh-huh. So, you'd better just tell me."

"I want to be with Madison when she has her baby. Silly, isn't it?"

"I don't think it's silly at all. She's your sister."

"I know, but I've got work and it isn't safe and…"

"Shhh…it's alright, my love. If this is what you need, then do it."

"I can't just go, Ben."

"Of course, you can. I'll arrange for you to have a few days off at the hospital. Will that help?"

"I can't ask you to do that. Imagine how the tongues will wag. The other residents will have a pissy fit. It's bad enough that I'm sleeping with the drop-dead gorgeous 'boss'. This will really get up their noses."

"You're so good for my ego," Ben chuckled. "They're adults, darling. They're just going to have to get over themselves and deal with it. Besides, do you really give a crap what they think?"

"No, I suppose not."

I bit my lip again.

"You're worried about Mateo, aren't you?"

"How can I afford not to? I don't trust the silence, Ben. I was convinced that he'd be waiting in the wings, hiding somewhere in the shadows, just waiting for me to slip up."

Ben's expression changed. It was subtle but I immediately picked up on it. I'd honed my body language reading skills while I was with Mateo. It's vital to be able to read someone when your rib cage depended on it.

"What aren't you telling me, Benjamin Forbes?"

"Okay, don't get mad."

"Oh, Ben. What did you do?"

"Nothing crazy. Remember when we were at the cabin, I told you I had a contact?"

"Yes, I remember."

"I called him a few weeks ago."

"What did you tell him?"

"I explained our situation to him."

My anxiety levels were through the roof while I waited for Ben to tell me what he'd discussed with his contact.

"His name is Sam. He and I served together in the military. He owns a security and investigations company here in New York. I told him that we're worried about Mateo, and he called one of his contacts in Mexico who is now surveilling Mateo."

I got up and went to the open-plan kitchen for a drink of water. My mouth was so dry, it felt as if I had been sucking on cotton balls.

"At least we know where he is now, Peyton."

I gulped down some water and returned to my seat in the living room.

"You're saying someone is watching him?"

"Yes. Twenty-four-seven, my love. And Sam promised to keep me in the loop at all times."

I felt strangely at peace for the first time since I left Mexico. Was it true? Was it time to relax a bit and not worry my ass off from dawn to dusk, looking in the rearview mirror for that face that haunted my dreams?

"Thank you, Ben," I said softly, more under my breath than out loud.

"I told you he wouldn't hurt you anymore. I'm here, Peyton. I'm looking out for you and will continue to do so for the rest of my life."

I threw my arms around my lover's neck and held him closely.

"So, you see, if you want to go and be with Madison when she gives birth to your niece, you should do so. I'll hold the fort back here at home. How long do you want to be there?"

"A week should be plenty. Madison is due any day now."

"Done."

"I love you, Ben. What would I do without you?"

"Let's hope you never have to find out," he grinned.

* * *

I didn't tell my family I was coming. I wanted it to be a surprise. Ben dropped me off at the airport and watched until I was safely on the plane. I was much more at ease than the last time I'd ventured out of New York City.

At first, I was mad at Ben for telling Sam about Mateo. But, as I had time to think it over, I realized what an angel he was for doing so. The thought that someone knew where my husband was at all times was the catalyst I needed to start living like someone who'd been freed from her cage.

The plane landed at 7 pm. I decided to call a cab to take me to Madison's house, but when I put my phone back on, I had a message from Mom telling me that my sister had gone into labor that afternoon and that she and her husband, Craig, were at the hospital. I couldn't believe how perfect the timing of my visit was.

I called a cab and told the driver to take me straight to the hospital.

I went straight to reception and asked which room she was in. A bouncy orderly showed me to the floor that she was on and soon I could hear the moans of a woman in active labor coming from one of the delivery rooms. I popped my head around the door.

"Peyton!" Madi yelled at the top of her voice between her Lamaze breathing.

"Hey, you," I grinned. What's all this noise? You'd think that someone was having a baby."

"What are you doing here?" her husband asked me with a smile and hugged me.

"Someone has to give Madi a hand once yours is crushed.

"I can't believe it," Madi said, with tears in her eyes.

I walked over to her bed and held her hand.

"Surprise," I chuckled.

"Ooph! Hee…hee…hee…hoo…hoo…hoo… Ouch, that was a big one," she moaned through her tears.

"Does Mom know you're here?"

"Not yet. Where is she?"

"She's watching the boys," her husband answered and wiped Madi's forehead with a damp cloth.

"Can I get you some ice chips, Sis?" I asked.

Madison was breathing hard. She nodded.

I left the room for a moment and went to the ice machine. I had mixed emotions about being there with Madi. Sorrow over the baby I'd lost, and joy for the new life my sister was about to bring into the world.

I stood at the ice machine for a while so I could compose myself. The day belonged to Madison and her husband. I wasn't going to dampen their joy and excitement by crying over my particular pint of spilled milk.

Craig looked rather stressed when I returned to the room.

"Do you want to grab a quick cup of coffee, Craig? I'll stay here with Madi," I offered.

"Do you mind, babe?" he asked Madison.

"No, it's fine."

"Okay, great. I need to make a few calls quickly. I'll be right back, angel. You're doing brilliantly. I love you. Thank you, Peyton."

"No problem."

"How are you, Sis?" Madi asked once Craig was out of earshot.

"All good, Madi."

"I can't believe you're here," she said again. "Thank you so much for coming."

"Of course. I'm just glad I made it. I got the message from Mom when I switched my phone back on after the flight landed. Talk about a close call."

"I think Gabi must have known you were coming," Madi laughed.

"Or something like that."

I dipped the cloth into cold water and wiped down my sister's sweaty brow. How far apart are the contractions?"

"About three minutes. She's in a rush, alright."

"I'd say your baby girl is an overachiever like her mom. She's early, isn't she?"

"Yeah. A few days. This is new for me. The boys were late."

"Sounds about right," I laughed. "Gabi is keen to get into that fort. I hope her brothers are ready for her. If she's a true Taylor she's going to make them sit up and pay attention from the get-go."

"Here comes another one," Madi groaned before she launched into another psychoprophylactic breathing session.

"Holy, crap! That was the worst one yet. Come on, Gabi, it's time, my darling. Let's get you out of there and into the world," she said to her contorted belly.

A nurse came into the room, checked the monitor reading, and smiled at us.

"I'm going to do a quick internal check to see how far you've dilated, Mrs. Theron."

"Hi," I said. "I'm her sister, Peyton."

"Hello, Peyton. I'm Nurse Rogers. Pleased to meet you."

"Peyton's a doctor," Madi announced proudly.

"Oh? Well, that's a good thing. We can never have too many eyes on the prize," the nurse smiled. I like her. She was sweet.

"Okay. You're there. Ten centimeters," she said. "I'm going to rally the troops quickly," she said and left the room.

I didn't want to be on the business end of the birthing. I was there to support Madi.

"I'm going to pop out for a second and find Craig," I said and kissed Madi on her cheek.

"Thanks, Sis."

I made my way to the coffee shop I'd passed on my way in. Craig was pacing up and down, talking to someone on his phone. I nodded when he looked up and saw me, at which point he ended the call and walked toward me.

"It's time, Daddy," I grinned. "You'd better get in there."

"Thanks, Peyton. I'm so happy you're here."

"I'm glad too, Craig," I said and watched as he ran back toward Madi's delivery room.

At that moment I wondered what my life would have been like had I given birth to my daughter. Would it have been hard raising her by myself? They say things happen for a reason. I kept telling myself that, over and over, to ease the pain of such a great loss.

My thoughts brought me back to Mateo. All my mental paths seemed to end up at his doorstep. I decided to give Madi and Craig their privacy. The miracle of birth was a celebration for expectant parents, and I wasn't going to be the third wheel.

My stomach made a hollow noise, and I realized that I hadn't eaten since breakfast. I'd been too nervous about the trip to eat on the plane. I entered the coffee shop and had a look at the overhead menu.

I ordered a cheeseburger and sat down at a table. My phone rang. It was my mom. She was probably worried about me seeing as I hadn't called her back. I'd been so caught up in Madi's labor that I forgot.

"Hey, Mom."

"Peyton. I was worried when I didn't hear back from you. Are you alright?"

"Sorry for not calling you back. I'm great, thanks, Mom."

"Madi's in labor, sweetheart. Dad and I are watching the boys while she and Craig are at the hospital."

"Yeah, I know. Guess where I am."

"Where?"

"I'm at the coffee shop in the hospital while Madi is busy pushing."

"What?!"

"Surprise," I laughed.

"Oh, my goodness. What a wonderful day."

"I was on the plane when you left the message. I came straight to the hospital when I got your message. In all the excitement I completely forgot to call you back."

"Ah, Pey, my darling, I'm so happy. You say Madi is giving birth."

"Yes. I left her and Craig in the delivery room. Didn't want to be the third wheel."

"Wonderful. Are you coming here tonight?"

"I think I'll stay here and come over in the morning. Is that alright?"

"Of course. I'll see you in the morning. Oh, Peyton. I'm so happy. I love you, darling. See you soon."

"I love you, Mom. See you in the morning. Love to Dad and the boys."

22

BEN

Was that the phone ringing? I was somewhere between sleep and awake, so it took me a few seconds to open my eyes and find the bloody device. I could see the light shining through the blankets. Got it.

It was 2 am. What the hell?

"Hello," I answered in a groggy voice.

"Ben, it's Sam."

The sound of his voice was like falling through a crack in the ice and hitting the sub-zero water beneath. I was instantly awakened.

"What happened? What's wrong?"

"My contact just called me. He lost sight of Mateo, and no one knows where he is."

"What the fuck? Are you sure?"

"I'm sure."

"How long ago did he vanish?"

"A few hours ago. Is Peyton with you?"

Oh, fuck! Peyton!

"No. She's with her family. Her sister is having a baby. The timing couldn't be worse, Sam!"

"Look, I'm not saying this is a catastrophe, but I suggest you call Peyton and warn her to be careful. If he is on his way to The States, he may be looking for trouble."

"Okay, thanks for calling, Sam. Let me know if your man finds him."

"Will do. I'm sorry about this, Ben. I don't know how, but he must have spotted our man."

"I'll talk to you later."

I ended the call and immediately dialed Peyton's number. The call went straight to voicemail. She was probably asleep. Damn it! I got up and went straight to my computer. If Mateo was on his way to Peyton's folks, I'd have to get there as soon as possible.

I pulled up the list of available flights to Peyton's hometown so I could get the hell over there as soon as possible. I could only pray that I'd get there in time.

I found a flight scheduled to leave in an hour and a half and booked a seat on it. I threw a few items of clothing in a bag and headed for the airport.

I drove like the devil was chasing after me. All I could think of was Peyton and how I would warn her. I tried a few times to call her phone but without luck.

"Pick up, Peyton!" I yelled at the cell phone and threw it down onto the passenger's seat.

Calm down, Ben. No sense in getting yourself all worked up into a frenzy. She's with her family. She's probably sleeping. Get on the plane and then you can quietly lose your shit.

181

I left my car in an undercover parking bay, locked it, and rushed to board the plane. I could have scaled the wall and snapped the overhead announcement board in half when the words 'flight delayed' flashed across the screen.

I made my way through the throngs of passengers to the counter and spoke to the boarding assistant.

"Excuse me, do you know what the delay is?" I asked her.

"There's quite a bad storm overhead, Sir," she smiled, trained to keep her game face on at all times. "The flight should be here in the next half an hour. We do apologize for the inconvenience. Perhaps you could enjoy a coffee while you wait."

I was sorely tempted to tell her where she could shove her coffee, but I understood that it wasn't her fault that Mateo had disappeared from sight or that Peyton wasn't answering her phone. Neither could the poor girl control the weather overhead. I had no other option but to find a seat somewhere and try calling Peyton again.

Peyton had given me her parents' home number once, in case I ever needed it. I looked at my watch. It was the middle of the night. Was it wise to call there and whip the whole family into a frenzy? Probably not.

Mateo hadn't been gone for too long. I calculated the time it would take him to travel from Mexico City to the border. By my calculations, it would take him roughly six and a half hours to get there, and then about an hour to get to Peyton.

I would get to her about an hour before he did if the fucking plane would get its ass in gear. Then again, I didn't know when he'd left Mexico City, so basically, I could have done all the calculations in the world and still come up clueless. Fuck! Where was the plane?

The flight landed an hour later than the booking assistant had calculated. I was a fuming mess by the time we boarded. To add insult to injury, I sat next to a woman with a baby who screamed throughout the flight. I was ready to murder by the time I stepped onto terra firma.

It was morning, and the sun was beating down on my head. I booked an Uber as soon as I stepped into the airport building and typed in Peyton's parents' address. The car and driver arrived a few minutes later.

"Hello," the young man greeted me with a pleasant smile.

"I'm in a hurry," I said and threw my bag into the trunk of the car. "Step on it. I'll pay the fines."

The driver nodded and got behind the wheel.

Hang in there, Peyton. I'm on my way.

* * *

The nurse who tended to Madi was kind enough to provide me with a bed for the night. I supposed she thought she'd extend a fellow professional a courtesy. I was grateful for it.

I woke up just before dawn and checked in with my sister and her beautiful new baby girl. Gabi was a beautiful baby with perfect fingers and toes, and a peaceful little face. She looked like Madi. I was both envious and overjoyed.

"Hey, Madi," I whispered when I walked into her room and saw her breastfeeding the hungry little mouth.

"Hi, Pey. Isn't she just adorable?" she asked with a look of complete joy on her face.

"She's the prettiest baby I've ever seen, Sis. And, trust me, I've seen a few."

"I can't believe she's finally here. Would you like to hold her?"

"And interrupt her tasty breakfast? No way."

"I meant after her feed, silly."

"I'd love to. Where's Craig?"

"He's gone home for an hour or so. He'll bring the boys back with him. I'm sure they're dying to see their sister."

"I suppose Mom and Dad will come then, too."

"Yeah."

"I'm all sticky. I think I'll pop over to Mom and Dad's for a shower and then come back with them."

"That's a good idea. Perhaps you can hold Gabi then."

"I think so. I wouldn't want our first meeting to be one where I'm all sticky and smelly," I grinned.

"Hey, you couldn't be any worse than her brothers," Madi laughed.

"Good point. I'll see you in a bit, Sis. Congrats again. She's exquisite," I said and kissed my sister on the forehead.

"Thanks, Pey. You're next," she whispered.

"You bet."

I left mother and daughter to snuggle and called an Uber. I was looking forward to a long, warm soak in the tub and mom's infamous, artery clogging, bacon and eggs breakfast. Outside, dawn was breaking, coloring the sky in stunning orange hues. I took in a deep breath and turned my face to the rising sun.

How wonderful it had been to share the auspicious occasion with Madison and Craig. I was happy.

The Uber driver pulled up outside the hospital.

"Good morning, Dr. Taylor," he greeted.

"Hi, Derek."

"May I take your bag?" he asked and reached for it.

"Uh, no, it's fine. Thanks."

I got into the car and soon we were on our way to Mom and Dad's, turned my phone on and texted Mom.

> *Hey, Mom. Catching an Uber home. Dying for a good breakfast. Do you mind whipping up a Taylor special for me?*

Mom texted back.

> *Good morning, sweetheart. Would you mind stopping at the store on your way and grabbing us some eggs? Dad and I are almost home from Madi's place and I'm not sure I have enough.*

I texted again.

> *Sure, thing. See you in a bit.*
> *Love you.*

"Uh, Derek. Would you mind terribly stopping off at the store for me? I'll throw in a little extra for your trouble. I'll be two minutes."

"Sure, Doc. No problem."

"Thank you so much."

My phone suddenly died. The damn battery was flat. In all the excitement I'd forgotten to charge the bloody thing. I made a mental note to do so as soon as I arrived home so I could call Ben and tell him the good news. He was probably sleeping in any way, so no harm done.

The Uber driver stopped at a market near my folks. I jumped out of the car with my wallet in hand and walked toward the greengrocer. My nose led me straight to a coffee vendor where I ordered a double cappuccino.

"I'll grab it on the way out of the store," I told the barista, who nodded and took the cash.

I bought some eggs and added a few fresh croissants too. My mouth was watering when I left the store, so I pulled a piece of croissant out of the bag and popped the buttery morsel into my mouth. It tasted good, so I went in for another piece.

My cappuccino was waiting for me by the time I got back to the barista.

"Oohh, thank you," I purred and took the cup from him.

"Have a good day," he smiled.

Freshly brewed coffee and warm croissants. What a way to start my day. Could I be any happier?

"Hello, dear," I heard an unexpected voice behind me.

The tiny hair on the back of my neck shot up, and my mouth grew instantly dry, so much so that I couldn't swallow the food in my mouth. I felt something hard poking me in the small of my back.

I dropped the bag and heard the eggs inside shatter as they hit the concrete. My legs were lame. No matter how much I wanted to run, I couldn't move.

"So nice to see you," the voice continued.

"Mateo," I whispered with a shaky voice.

I tried to turn around, but he wouldn't let me.

"Walk," he barked.

Did I run? Did I scream?

"I know what you're thinking, bitch," Mateo growled again. "Don't try anything. I'm holding a gun to your back. It has a silencer on it, so no one will hear a thing if I pull the trigger. Walk!"

"Mateo, please…"

Mateo pushed the silencer roughly into my spine. I whimpered as the barrel dug into the skin.

"Okay," I said, hoping to pacify him.

How the fuck did he find me?

I looked around to see if I could get anyone's attention, but it was early and there weren't many people out and about. I wondered if the Uber driver could see me. Would he get out of the car and help me if I made a gesture for help? Would Mateo kill him and then me if he tried?

"Where are we going?" I asked.

"That black SUV in the last bay," Mateo instructed.

His voice was cold—colder than I remembered. Had he been following the Uber? I was so busy chatting with Mom and thinking of my stomach, I wasn't paying attention to the cars behind us.

"Get in," Mateo said and pushed me into the car once he'd opened the back door.

I knocked my knee as I fell into the vehicle. I rubbed at the site of the throbbing pain. Out of the corner of my eye, I saw Mateo reach into his pocket. He pulled out a syringe and jammed it into my leg.

"Ouch! What the fu…" I yelled, but the world around me went dark before I could finish my sentence.

23

BEN

I was on high alert when the Uber pulled up outside Peyton's parents' house. I asked the driver to wait for me, just in case Peyton was elsewhere.

I walked along the line of perfectly pruned rose bushes to the front door of the home and rang the bell. The door opened a few moments later. The woman standing before me had an excited look on her face that soon changed to one of confusion. It was clear that she was expecting someone else. Peyton perhaps?

"Hello," she greeted. "Can I help you?"

Of course. She didn't know me. For all intents and purposes, I was a stranger on her doorstep.

"Hello," I said and smiled. "My name is Ben. Is Peyton here?"

"O.o.o.h. Ben. Hi. This is a surprise. I'm Millie, Peyton's mom. Please, come in."

"Thank you," I said but stayed where I was. "Is she here?"

"No, not yet. But she's on her way from the hospital. Her sister gave birth to her baby daughter last night. Peyton stayed with her."

"That's wonderful, Millie. Congratulations. I tried to call Peyton on her phone but it's off."

I nodded and waved the Uber driver off.

"Her phone is probably flat. I'm sure she'll be here soon. May I offer you a cup of coffee? Peyton is bringing the eggs for a breakfast feast. Are you hungry?"

"Uh, no Thank you, I'm not hungry. But a cup of coffee would be lovely, thank you."

"Frank!" Millie called, "Come and meet Ben."

I heard footsteps coming toward us.

"Goodness, what a pleasant surprise. Hello, Ben. Good to meet you. Frank Taylor," Peyton's father said and extended his hand.

"It's a pleasure to meet you, Frank," I said and shook his hand.

"Does Peyton know you're here?"

"No, I thought I'd surprise her," I lied.

There was no sense in alarming Peyton's folks unnecessarily. They'd been to hell and back with Mateo. I was amazed they even let me in the door. Peyton must have told them that I wasn't a reprobate.

"Come in," Frank gestured.

I followed him to the living room and made myself comfortable on a sofa.

"How do you take your coffee, Ben?" Millie asked.

"Straight up, thank you. No milk or sugar."

"Would you like a cup, darling?" she asked Frank.

"I'd love one, thanks, my love."

"I believe congratulations are in order," I said to Frank.

"Oh, the baby. Yes, another grandbaby to keep Grandpa on his toes. Thank you. We watched over the boys last night while Madison went to the hospital. I must confess, I'm shattered," he whispered and grinned. "It's amazing how soon one forgets how busy little boys are when your own children are all grown up."

"They must treasure their grandparents."

"Do you have children?" he asked.

"No, but I'm looking forward to having a few one day."

"They're a handful alright, but well worth the effort. My girls are the light of my life."

I watched as Frank's eyes clouded over for a brief moment as if he were thinking of something painful, he'd sooner forget.

"Anyway," he said, "does Pey know you're here? She didn't mention it to her mother and me."

"No, I was just telling Millie I decided to surprise her."

"I see."

"Here you go," Millie interrupted and handed me a mug of coffee and then gave one to her husband.

"Thank you."

I took a few sips of coffee and then looked at my watch. I'd been at the house for almost fifteen minutes. No Peyton.

Millie must have seen me checking the time.

"I wonder what's keeping Peyton," she said.

"Why don't you call her, darling?"

"Ben says her phone is off."

"Perhaps Peyton told Madi where she was going before coming here. You know our girls, Love. Shopping, shopping, shopping," Frank grinned. "Call Madi. Peyton would have told her sister for sure."

"That's a good idea. I'll call Madi. Who knows, perhaps she stopped to buy the baby and the boys a gift before she sees them."

"I wouldn't be too surprised."

I prayed that Peyton's parents were right in their assumptions. It was better than the alternative dashing about like a wrecking ball in my mind.

Millie was out of the room for a few minutes. My coffee was almost done by the time she came back, and my stomach had an awful hollow feeling that wouldn't settle, despite the dark liquid swirling about inside of it. Something wasn't right.

"And? What did Madi say?" Frank asked his wife.

"She said Peyton didn't say anything to her about stopping off anywhere. I did ask her to buy some eggs. She must have gotten side-tracked. She does know scores of people in town. She could have stopped for a quick catch-up with one of her friends."

I couldn't ignore the nagging feeling that something terrible had happened to Peyton. I had to say something to her parents, but my delivery of the bad news was crucial. I didn't want to scare them.

"There's something I need to tell you," I started. "I didn't want to say anything, but I'm very worried."

Frank and Millie stared silently at me. I could see the color draining from their faces. Frank was the first one to respond.

"Why? What's wrong, Ben?"

"Peyton told me everything about what Mateo put her and her family through. She and I have grown very close in the past few months, as I'm sure she's told you."

"Yes," Millie said, "and we're very grateful for you, Ben."

"I love your daughter very much, Millie, so I asked an ex-military friend of mine, Sam, who owns a security company, to keep an eye on Mateo."

"I see," Frank said.

"He's been watching him for a few weeks now," I continued. "However, Sam called me last night and told me that Mateo has disappeared. No one has seen him. That's why I'm here."

"Oh, no!" Millie gasped.

"Do you think he's coming here?" Frank asked, looking terribly worried.

"I don't know. But I'd rather be safe than sorry, so I flew here as soon as I could."

Millie looked at her watch again, and then at her husband.

"She should have been here by now, Frank," she said in a shaky voice.

"Ben," Frank said and got up, "let's go for a drive."

"Find her, Frank," Millie said with tears welling up in her beautiful blue eyes.

"We'll find her, sweetheart," he said and kissed her on the forehead.

I followed Frank to the garage where we got into his car.

"Oh, Frank!" Millie called after us. "Peyton said she was in an Uber when she texted me."

"Great. Thanks, hon. I'll call the service and see if I can find out which driver picked her up," I said.

"Okay. Call me as soon as you find her, please."

"Will do, Millie," Frank said and pressed the button which opened the automated garage door.

I googled the nearest Uber while Frank was reversing out of the garage. As soon as I had the number, I called the helpline and explained our situation to the dispatcher. Of course, they were of no use, stating they couldn't give us any information due to privacy concerns, blah, blah, blah. I was furious but it made no difference to the end result.

"I'll drive to the nearest greengrocer where we usually buy our eggs," Frank said. "Let's ask around if anyone's seen her there."

"That's a good idea, Frank."

I called Sam while Frank drove.

"Ben. Any news?"

"No. I'm with Peyton's father. It's not looking good, Sam. No one has seen her, and her phone is off."

"Shit! Can I help?"

"Yeah, I called Uber to find out where the driver stopped with Peyton, but they won't give me any information."

"Yeah, they're pretty strict about giving out their info. Leave it with me. Where was the pickup?"

Frank gave me the address of the hospital, and I relayed it to Sam.

"I'll call you back," Sam said and hung up.

Damn it, Peyton. Where are you?!

The shopping center where Frank drove us to was busy by the time we got there. He parked and then we got out of the car and walked around.

First, we went to the greengrocer. Frank chatted to the sales assistant, who then asked the teller if she had seen a woman fitting Peyton's description. The young girl remembered Peyton because they chatted for a bit about the free-range chicken farm where the eggs were from.

"Yeah," she said with a bouncy disposition, "she was here about an hour ago."

"Do you happen to know if she was alone?" I asked.

"Sorry, I wasn't paying attention. I think so, though."

"Okay, thanks."

"Hang on," the girl said as I was walking away. "She did say she was sorry for paying me in change. She said the barista gave her coins when she bought a coffee."

"Barista?"

"Yeah. He's got a little coffee cart around the corner."

"Thank you very much," Frank said.

"Sure thing. I hope you find her. She's a nice lady."

Frank and I headed in the direction that the teller pointed us and soon found the coffee cart.

"Excuse me," I said to the young man.

"Yeah, what's your poison man?" he grinned. "No, let me guess. Double espresso?" he grinned.

"No, thanks. I'm looking for someone."

"Hey, aren't we all, buddy?" he laughed.

I took out my cell phone and showed him a picture of Peyton.

"Oh, yeah. Early bird. Nice lady. Double cappuccino."

"Okay. Did you see which way she went?"

"Uhm…let me think. Oh, yeah, she went that way," he said and pointed. "She's a bit clumsy, though. Dropped her eggs on the ground. Her man looked a little pissed at her, poor thing."

"Her man? What man?" I asked, feeling the energy draining from my body as the shock of his words started to sink in.

"The guy who joined her after I gave her the coffee."

"What did he look like?" Frank asked.

"Tall guy, dark hair, good looking."

Fuck, no! Mateo!

"They left in an SUV."

Frank and I looked at each other and moved as fast as we could to get back to the car.

"Mateo?" I asked.

"Mateo," Frank nodded. "We have to call the cops."

"I don't think that's going to do us any good, Frank. Mateo is Peyton's husband. They'll tell us to wait forty-eight hours. I'll call Sam. He'll know what to do."

My phone rang as soon as I took it out of my pocket. It was Sam.

"Okay, Ben, I spoke to the driver. He said…."

"It's too late, Sam. He's got her."

"Fuck. Okay, the driver told me she never came back from the greengrocer."

"I know. We just spoke to someone who saw her getting into an SUV with someone who fits Mateo's description. Fuck, Sam! I'm going to drop Peyton's father off at home and drive to Mexico."

"No! Ben, listen to me. You can't go alone. You have no idea what you're going to walk into. It may be a trap. Come home and we'll put together a team."

"There's no time for that, Sam! He has her. God knows what he's planning on doing to her. He's a psychopath!"

"Captain Forbes!"

The sound of Sam's yelling snapped me out of my panic.

"Listen to me," he carried on. "Stay where you are. I'm coming. I'll bring a team of men with me. In the meanwhile, stay with Peyton's family. They may be in danger. Do you copy?"

"Fine," I said, reluctantly. "I'll send you an address."

"Hang in there, soldier. See you in a bit."

"Sam," I said before he hung up.

"Yeah, buddy?"

"Pack me a weapon."

24

PEYTON

U*gh...my head hurts. Where am I? What is that awful smell? How...*

My eyes shot open. I tried to sit up a few seconds later. Oh, no. No, no, no...I knew exactly where I was without having to look around. The fucking basement! I was back in Mexico City—correction, back in hell!

To say that I was terrified was an epic understatement. My body was ice cold and try as I might, I couldn't budge. Mateo had tied me to a bed. The son of a bitch had appeared when I'd least expected it, and now I was going to pay dearly for my mistake. The only question was, how much?

"Mateo!" I screamed, knowing full well that he couldn't hear me. "Mateo! Where are you, you fucking coward?" I screamed again, more for my own benefit than anything else. The action made me feel tougher than I was, which, granted, wasn't very much at all.

My leg was hurting in the spot where my psycho husband had jabbed me with a needle. Suffice it to say Mateo hadn't employed any finesse, unsurprisingly. I couldn't even rub the spot as my hands were tied.

Well done, Peyton. This time you are truly and royally fucked!

I wondered how long Mateo was planning on leaving me there, twisting in the wind, dreading his intentions. Being tied to a bed like a dog was likely a small part of the elaborate punishment to follow.

Damn it! Why did I think it was safe to leave Ben behind and venture out on my own? My family was probably sick with worry, wondering where I'd gotten off to. Were they frantic by now? And Ben. Did he even know that I was in danger? What a mess.

I lay there for what seemed like hours before I heard the sound of a key turning in the lock. My whole being turned rigid with fear. Was this the end? I heard deliberate footsteps as Mateo descended the staircase. The plan now was to keep my face free from any trace of panic. It wasn't going to be easy.

"Ah, mi amor," he mocked.

"Fuck you," I said calmly, without raising my voice.

"I see your time away has done nothing to improve your manners," he smirked.

"A little hypocritical of you, don't you think, you murderous psycho?"

"Ouch," he countered, sarcastically, and placed his hand over his black heart. As if anyone could actually hurt him.

"Congratulations, Mateo. So, you found me. Now what?"

"Slow down, darling," he grinned and stroked my hair. "No need to rush into anything. I have a few questions, first."

"Ha! You have questions!" I snarled and tried my best to pull away from his touch.

"You'll get your turn. As I said, this isn't a sprint."

I couldn't imagine what Mateo thought he'd accomplish by asking me questions, but I wanted to stall my imminent death, so I had no option but to humor him for the time being.

"What do you want to know?" I acquiesced.

"Where is my child?"

My temper hit the roof in about a nanosecond at that incredulous question. His child! How dare he claim someone he didn't want. But I had to keep calm, so I took in a few deep breaths before I answered.

"*My* child is dead, thanks to you. You killed her when you threw me down the stairs. Remember that? Or were you too drunk?"

"No, I remember," he barked.

I recognized the warning signs hidden in the tone of his voice, but I didn't care at that point. My heart was filled with rage over my murdered daughter.

"What? Are you waiting for an apology?" he sniped. "I told you I didn't want a fucking kid."

"And you couldn't have discussed that with me beforehand? Before we got married?"

"If you had taken the pill like you were supposed to, we wouldn't be in this situation now, would we?"

"Are you fucking listening to yourself? I *was* on the pill! It's not one hundred percent effective, you know. It wasn't as if I wanted to bring a child into this farce of a marriage. All you had to do was divorce me, Mateo. You didn't have to try and kill me and our child."

"No one leaves me, Peyton, or hasn't your clever little brain worked that out yet?"

"So, that's it. If you can't have me, no one else can. Is that the tired old stereotype?"

"Where have you been hiding all this time?" Mateo asked, changing the subject.

Good! He didn't know where I lived. He didn't know about Ben!

Thank you, God!

"How did you find me?" I asked instead, avoiding his question.

"I told you. You'll have your turn to ask questions. Answer me!" he growled.

"Boston," I lied.

"And who in Boston are you fucking?"

"No one. I've had my fill of men, thank you."

"Please. Bitches like you need a man in their lives."

"What do you mean, bitches like me?"

"Nesters. You want the white picket fence and the two-point-five, snot nosed kids running around the house."

"Wow! Why do you hate kids so much, Mateo?"

"They fuck everything up, that's why," he snarled.

"What's the matter? Did mommy not love you enough? Too much? Did she tell you that you ruined her life? Cause I can see how she'd have a point, there."

I was taking a dangerous chance. Employing amateur psychiatry must have struck a nerve because the next thing I knew, Mateo slapped me so hard across the face that my vision blurred.

"That bitch wasn't fit to carry the title of mother!" he shouted.

Mateo's face genuinely scared the shit out of me at that point. Had I pushed him too far? I had to calm him down if I was going to make it through the night. But how?

"What did 'mommy the monster' do to you, my love?" I asked, hoping for the best.

"Don't try and sweet talk me, Peyton," he growled, but, at least the murderous crazy eyes were gone for the moment.

"I'm sorry. What did she do to hurt you?"

"It doesn't matter now. The whore got what she deserved."

Oh, Lord. What did he do to his mother? Is she down here somewhere in a bottle too?

If I was going to wiggle my way out of this trap, I'd have to change tactics.

"How did you know I'd be with Madison?"

Mateo's face changed once again. This was clearly a subject that he'd enjoy boasting over. He wore his smug smile once more.

"The PI I employed to find you, told me your sister was having a baby. I knew you couldn't resist being with her when she gave birth. You being a nester and all."

"Very clever."

My bladder was about to explode. I wondered if Mateo would be human enough to allow me to urinate with dignity. It was worth a shot.

"I need the bathroom, Mateo."

"Who's stopping you?"

"Untie me, please."

"Yeah, I don't think so, sweetheart."

"Come on, Mateo. Surely you don't expect me to wet myself?"

"Darling, I don't care if you crap your pants. You're not going anywhere."

His phone rang whilst I was formulating my verbal assault. But I wouldn't have the chance to utter my well-thought-out snipe because he answered the call and proceeded to leave.

"Wait! Mateo!" I screamed after him, but it was no use. He placed his hand over the speaker, glowered at me, and then ascended the stairs.

"Fuck! Come back! Mateo!"

Ah, screw it. I shifted my body so that my backside was on the edge of the bed and let my bladder go. What else was I going to do? All I could do was pray that someone would find me and release me from my hell.

So, this is what it was like to have urine-soaked clothes. No wonder babies put up such a stink between diaper changes.

Congratulations, Mateo. If scaring me half to death and humiliating me to within an inch of my life was part of your plan, then you've accomplished your mission. You rat bastard!

* * *

The whore was back! What a coup! I could have danced a jig at the look of utter shock on Peyton's face when I pushed her into my car and jabbed the needle into her thigh.

My wife looked good. Then again, she was the most beautiful woman I'd ever been with. Not that her beauty bought her any brownie points with me now. I saw past her tight ass and voluptuous tits and into her deceiving heart.

I didn't believe her for a second when she said she hadn't been with another man. Peyton was too stunning to be single. After I'd killed her slowly, I planned on finding the bastard and doing away with him too.

No one leaves Mateo Garcia, damn it!

My bitch mother thought it okay when she dropped me at the steps of the orphanage when she'd had enough of playing mommy. It had been for the best I supposed, as she was far too busy entertaining a succession of men to care for or about me.

But, I fixed her. Mommy dearest thought her fake tears of remorse would save her from my wrath. Stupid whore. I felt nothing when I plunged the knife into her cold heart and watched as she gasped and pissed herself while the life oozed out of her, red and sticky. The picture of her lifeless face was forever etched in the pathways of my brain.

Peyton had about as much chance of changing her fate as my mother had. She humiliated me and that was her mistake. She should have stayed and perhaps we'd have worked something out.

I left her in the basement to meet with a client and run a few errands. It was about 5 pm when I returned to the house. I imagined that Peyton had pissed herself by then, so I went to her cupboard and pulled out a clean pair of jeans and a blanket.

She was going to be my 'houseguest' for a while longer, so there was no sense in assaulting my senses in the process. I wanted Peyton to appreciate the error of her ways before I killed her. She was probably hungry, so I stopped in the kitchen and made her a sandwich before I went downstairs to the basement.

The faint smell of urine met me as I moved closer to where my wife was tied to the bed. She was startled when I dropped a bucket on the floor.

"There. No need to piss yourself again."

"How thoughtful," she snapped.

I walked over to her, cut the cable tie off her wrists, and placed one of her wrists in handcuffs. I closed the other cuff around the metal base of the bed so that Peyton wouldn't run.

"What do you want, Mateo?" she asked. "If you're trying to scare and humiliate me, you've accomplished your goal. Kudos. How much more are you wanting from me? You've already killed my child and possibly ruined my chances of ever being a mother. What more can you take from me?"

"You don't get it, do you?"

"Clearly not. Why don't you explain it to me?"

"Oh, I intend to. But I find action speaks louder than words, darling. And, when I'm done, you're going to appreciate the true meaning behind my sentiment."

"Did you ever love me, Mateo? Do you even understand what it means to love?"

"Ha! Please! Love. Phhh! There is no such thing. It's a fantasy society conjured up so that grown men give away everything they slave so hard for so that women can lord it over them. Love is bullshit, Peyton."

"I loved you," she said softly.

"No, you betrayed me. How is that love?"

I wanted to slap her when I saw the tears well up in her lying eyes.

"Here," I said and shoved the sandwich into her hand. "Eat this. You're going to need your strength.

25

BEN

Frank, Millie, Craig, Alyssa, and I were at the house, waiting for Sam and his men to arrive. We sat in the living room. Poor Millie was a wreck, and Frank was pacing up and down.

"I can't stand this waiting," he said and poured himself a whiskey. "I have to do something, Ben."

"Please, my love," Millie pleaded, "think of your heart."

"Stop fussing. I'm fine."

"It's going to be okay, Frank. Sam will be here soon, then we'll leave."

"How do we know that Mateo…"

Peyton's father couldn't finish his sentence, but we all knew what he was trying to say. None of us knew for sure that Peyton was still alive. I had to believe that Mateo would want to keep her alive so that he could 'teach her a lesson', as it were. Everything about the man screamed narcissist.

"I'll put on the kettle," Alyssa said and left the room.

I followed her. I needed some fresh air. We were all stressed to breaking point and waiting around had us all on the edge.

I hid my terror by falling back on my military training. I was never as thankful for that mental training as I was at that moment. No combat situation I'd ever been in could compare to the fear of losing Peyton.

"I still can't believe this is happening," Alyssa said while she and I were outside on the porch, drinking yet another cup of coffee. "I should have been with her. What the hell was I thinking, leaving her alone? I'm so glad you're here, Ben."

"I'm going to kill that bastard," was all I had to say.

"Promise me you'll make that Mateo louse suffer. He's taken so much from Peyton—from all of us—he has to account for his wickedness," she said with a shaky voice. She looked up at the sky and then whispered, "Oh, God, please let her be alive!"

"Don't allow your mind to go there, Alyssa. Peyton is a fighter, and she's smart. She will do what she has to do to stay alive. I believe that and so should you."

"You're right. I'm sorry," she said and wiped away a stream of tears.

"How are Madison and the baby?" I asked, hoping the subject change would temporarily distract the poor woman who was terrified at the prospect of losing her best friend.

"Madi's a wreck. Imagine it. This should have been one of the most exciting and happiest times in her and Craig's lives. She's just given birth to a baby girl, and now her sister is missing, kidnapped by a psychopath, no less."

"I'm going to get her back, Alyssa, or die trying. I promise."

"Thank you, Ben. I'm so sorry. I haven't even asked you how you're doing with all of this."

"Honestly, I'm as terrified as everyone here, but I intend on putting my training as a soldier to good use. I'm focusing on getting Peyton back home. Period. That's the only thing that's stopping me from coming apart at the seams."

"Peyton would be so proud of you, Ben. She's crazy about you, you know. I can see why."

"I love her very much."

"I know you do."

We stood there for a moment, neither one of us talking, looking out at the night sky.

"This is a beautiful place," I said.

"Yeah, it's peaceful, isn't it? Peyton loves the outdoors. She's always wanted to live on a ranch or somewhere in the mountains."

I remembered the conversation she and I had when we were at the cabin.

"Yes, she told me."

"A small-town doctor," she said. "That's what she dreams of being."

"Peyton is going to be a fine surgeon one day. Perhaps I can give her her dream. I'm certainly going to try."

My phone rang. It was Sam.

"We've just landed, Ben. See you soon."

Sam had access to a private jet, so there were no issues with flight delays. I was never more grateful for his contacts than I was at that moment.

"Okay. I'm on my way."

"Are they here?" Alyssa asked me once I'd ended the call.

"Yeah. They've just landed."

"Good. I'll take you to them."

"Mateo has a few hours of traveling time on us, so we'll leave as soon as possible. Feels like we're crawling toward Peyton's rescue. It's so fucking frustrating."

Alyssa brought the car around to the front while I said goodbye to the family.

"Bring my baby back to me, please, Ben," Millie pleaded.

"Of course," I said and hugged her.

"Thank you, Ben," Frank said and patted my shoulder.

Frank had begged me to come along, but I insisted he stay behind and protect his family. Who knew what Mateo had planned. After much fuss, he'd agreed to stay.

"Please, tell Madison not to worry, Craig."

"Thanks, Ben. Will do."

"I'll bring her back," I promised and got into the car.

* * *

It was just past midnight when we pulled into Mexico City.

"We need to stop off at a friend's," Sam announced. "He has put together a little goody bag for each of us."

"I hope it's a heavily ladened bag," I said.

"Oh, yes. Santiago doesn't fuck around when it comes to weapons. He isn't the number one gun store owner in the capitol for nothing."

"How do you know this guy?" I asked.

"He and I met at a weapons convention. He's a crazy mother fucker, but I wouldn't bet against him in a gunfight."

"Are you sure we can trust him, Sam?"

"Ben, I'd stake my life on it. He's as loyal as the day is long. Besides, he owes me a favor. It's a long story. I'll tell you over a beer someday."

"Deal."

Sam parked in a side street in an industrial-looking area.

"There's the back entrance to the store. Come along, Ben. Time to go shopping."

"I should have brought my fucking sword," I mumbled.

A bullet seemed far too impersonal considering the caliber of vermin we were hunting. I wanted to look Mateo square in the eye when I sent him off to his doom. But a gun made more sense under the circumstances.

Sam rapped his knuckles on the door. A stocky man with gold in his teeth opened and ushered us in. He led us to the back of the store and into an office.

"Sam, mi compadre," a man sitting on a desk called out happily.

"Santiago, you crazy Mexican bastard! How are you, pal?"

The two men embraced, slapped each other's backs, and laughed like best friends do.

"It's good to see you, Santiago, but we're going to have to catch up later. Ben here has a lady he needs to rescue."

"Si. I'm sorry to hear of your trouble, Ben," Santiago said in a thick accent. "Don't worry, I've got something here that will help you sort this asshole out," he said and pointed to a bag in the corner of the room.

"Ah! Excellent," Sam said and opened the bag.

"We're not robbing a bank, are we?" I asked when I saw the weapons.

"Maybe later," Santiago laughed.

"You're a pal," Sam said and closed the bag. "I'll get the ones we don't use back to you, buddy. The weapons that deliver the kill shots I'll dispose of."

"It's cool man. They're all clean. No one will trace them back to me."

"Thank you, Santiago," I said and shook his hand.

"Any friend of Sam's is a friend of mine," he smiled.

* * *

It was close to 2 am and the street on which Mateo lived was quiet.

"You think this guy knows we're coming?" Sam commented sarcastically while we watched two armed guards chatting at the entrance gate to the property.

"Wouldn't surprise me."

"Pete," Sam whispered to one of his men, "send up the drone."

We had to make certain that there weren't any surprises waiting for us on the other side of the wall.

Pete did as he was asked, and about ten minutes later, we were sure that there weren't more guards beyond the gate.

"Okay, boys. It's showtime," he whispered. "Remember, this scumbag has the Federales resident deep inside his asshole, so no screw-ups."

Everyone nodded. Sam and Pete moved stealthily toward the armed guards. The men didn't realize they were being stalked until it was too late. Two clean shots, delivered through silencer nozzles, took care of the immediate problem. The coast was clear.

Next, we had to work on the security system hurdle. I had no doubt that Mateo would have installed the best that money could buy. He wasn't exactly short of cash. What a shame it was that a man who had so much going for him would turn out to be such an evil bastard. Mateo could have been anything he wanted to be. But, instead, he chose to kill and destroy.

"Andrew, you're up," Sam waved.

Andrew scaled the wall like a cat, somehow avoided the electrified fencing, and made his way to a box near the gate. It took him roughly four minutes to bypass the security system once he'd unscrewed the cover plate. We were good to go.

The gates opened slowly.

"Let's go."

We knew there weren't any guards on the outside of the home, but we had no way of knowing if there were any bodyguards inside the house, so we had to move with caution.

Mateo's house was an homage to glass window makers everywhere. I imagined it must have been akin to living in a glass case. I guessed that he could keep an eye on his woman no matter where in the house she happened to be. No hiding from the master's beady eyes.

His vanity would prove to be his downfall, though, as it gave us the opportunity to see if he and Peyton were alone in there. We waited on the lawn for a few minutes to see if we could spot movement. It was quiet.

Sam and I made our way to a sliding door and checked it. Locked. That wasn't going to slow me down. I fiddled with the lock.

Sam handed me a gadget we'd learned to use in the military to bypass locks. I worked quickly and quietly until the handle moved freely under my hand. I opened the door and entered the house. Sam followed behind.

We split up and moved quietly in opposite directions. Where was Peyton? I could hear snoring coming from down the hall so I got down low and followed the sound.

"Hello!"

I spun around so fast I nearly tripped.

"Hello, handsome!"

What the fuck! A parrot! Peyton had never said anything about a parrot.

"Shut up," I whispered and moved to the fucking bird to throw a sheet over the cage.

"Give us a kiss!" the infernal bird shouted.

I reached out, grabbed a sheet, and threw it over the cage, to which the bird squawked unhappily. I wanted to wring its bloody neck. Had Mateo heard the racket? I didn't have to wait too long to find out. A noise behind me alerted me to the fact that someone was moving, clumsily, but quickly.

I turned to see a man, I assumed Mateo, running toward the kitchen. I followed as quickly as I could through the darkened passageway after him. He flung open a door and ran down a flight of stairs. I followed.

It was dark in the basement and the smell in there was one of death. I knew that smell all too well. Mateo was hovering over something. A bed. Peyton! She was cuffed to the frame of the bed, but she was alive.

"Ben!" she shouted when she saw me.

"Stay back or I'll slit her throat!" Mateo threatened.

Fuck!

26

PEYTON

"Ben!" I shouted again.

I couldn't believe my eyes. Was I having a dream? Was it a nightmare? Mateo had yanked me up off the bed and had a knife to my throat. I could feel the edge of the blade pressing against the skin which burned suddenly where the sharp metal was threatening to rip into flesh. I felt a trickle of blood running down to my collarbone.

"Let her go, Mateo!" Ben growled at the maniac behind me.

Mateo reeked of alcohol which made my situation even more precarious. One drunken slip and I'd be the third late Mrs. Garcia.

"Mateo, please," I begged in a calm voice, so as not to startle an already freaked-out madman.

"Shut up, you whore!" he yelled and hit me against the head with the butt of the knife.

It hurt like hell and left me seeing stars.

"Come on, you coward," Ben spat at Mateo. "Let her go and come over here so we can fight like men."

Mateo started cussing at Ben in Spanish. It was clear that he had no intention of doing the honorable thing. That didn't surprise me one bit. No, if I was going to make it out of this alive, I would have to employ the skills Ben had taught me. All I had to do was to wait for the right moment.

Mateo was close to hysteria. He was swaying and cursing, and I was terrified that he would lose control of the blade pressed against my throat. I could waste more time. It was now or never.

I took a deep breath and moved my right elbow backward and upward. The blow connected Mateo square in the jaw. He staggered back and fell onto the bed at which point I hunched down and out of his reach.

Ben leaped at the opportunity and lunged toward the bed where Mateo lay, momentarily dazed by my well-executed attack. Unfortunately, his confusion didn't last long and by the time Ben got to him, he was swinging the knife wildly. All I could do was watch as the blade cut into Ben's forearm.

I kept myself out of arm's length of the maniac who had once vowed to love, and cherish me, and watched as the two men struggled for the weapon. Ben moved lightning fast and punched Mateo in the throat at which point the latter dropped the knife and reached for his Adam's apple.

With one smooth move, Ben thrust the blade into Mateo's chest. And suddenly the fight was over. Mateo collapsed into a heap on the cold basement floor and Ben rushed over to where I cowered.

"Peyton, are you hurt?"

"Ben," was all I could utter before I passed out.

* * *

I was vaguely aware that I was in a moving vehicle. Was I in a car? I opened my eyes very slowly, praying that I wasn't hallucinating, caught up in some kind of delusional state where my mind was trying to overcome the trauma of being chained to a bed in the dungeon of death.

No, I was definitely in a car. A hand reached out and touched my arm.

"Shhh, it's okay. You're alright, my love."

"Ben?" I whispered.

"Yes, Peyton. It's me."

Ben's face slowly came into focus. His beautiful eyes were filled with concern.

"Are you feeling okay?" he asked.

"What happened?" I asked, trying to put together the pieces of the crazy puzzle.

"Mateo is dead. I'm taking you home."

"Dead?"

"Yes. You're safe now."

"Are you sure?"

"As sure as I'll ever be," he said and gently touched my face.

"Ugh! My head hurts."

"I'm not surprised. You've been through the mill."

I looked down at my clothes. They were clean.

"Oh, I took the liberty of changing you into fresh clothes."

"I smell awful," I said and looked at my dirty hands.

"You smell wonderful to me," Ben smiled.

"I can't believe you found me, Ben."

Then I remembered the deep gash Mateo had inflicted upon Ben's arm.

"How's your arm?"

"It will be fine. Don't worry about it."

"Oh, Ben."

The floodgates opened unexpectedly and out gushed fear, pain, regret, and finally tears of joy. I was free! Truly free from the monster who had enslaved not only my body but my mind for far too long.

"We're not out of the woods yet, my love," Ben said as he held my hand. I have to smuggle you out of Mexico now but don't worry. I have a plan.

"The Mexican police will be looking for us, Ben. Won't they?"

Mateo would have instructed his awful minions to look for me if anything happened to him. Of that I was certain. And, finding him stabbed to death in his home was a dead giveaway in my books.

"Eventually, yes. But, for now, they'll have to find Mateo's body, and trust me, that won't be easy."

I didn't want to know what Ben had done with Mateo's body. I didn't care, as callous as that may have appeared to the uninformed. I was free and we were on our way home. That was good enough for me.

"How did you find me, Ben?"

"I had some help. Sam and his boys came through for us, babe."

"How?"

I listened while Ben told me everything that had happened, starting at the point when he realized that Mateo had taken me and up to that of my escape.

"You are my hero, Ben Forbes," I smiled and lay my head against his shoulder.

"Oh, by the way," he said, "you didn't mention the pesky parrot to me. That was nearly a disaster."

"Parrot? What parrot?"

"The parrot that rather fancied me," he grinned.

"I have no idea what you're talking about. I can only imagine that Mateo must have been tired of arguing with himself," I said and rolled my eyes. "Either that or his next unsuspecting victim was a parrot fanatic."

* * *

"Are you comfortable?" Ben asked me before he closed the lid.

"Yeah, I'll be okay."

I was tucked away in a smallish box under the backseat of the car. The built-in box was snug, but I could breathe and if all went according to plan, cross the Mexican border back into the US without being detected. I had to admit that I was overjoyed that it would be the last time I was smuggled out of Mexico!

We'd stopped near the border post so that Ben could hide me from sight. I couldn't wait to get home. It would be a very long time before I'd travel anywhere again, on purpose, anyway.

Ben started up the engine and drove. I could hear his voice still, so he kept me posted as to how far away I was from freedom.

"Okay, I can see the queue. Not a peep now, my love."

My heart rate was soaring, but I tried to keep my breathing steady. The car slowed down and soon we were stationary.

Please, Lord. I promise never to come back to this Godforsaken place again. Just let me get home safely.

I heard the official's voice, very faintly, from my cocoon. Then I heard Ben's. It felt like we stood still for hours. Ben switched off the engine and then the car door opened, and someone ruffled around in the back of the vehicle.

Fuck, fuck, fuck...

If they found me, both Ben and I would rot away in a Mexican prison forever. I'd watched plenty of reality TV shows of people caught smuggling drugs. What would they do to a man who was smuggling the wife of a murdered man out of the country? Ben would get the chair for sure! What was taking so long?

The car door closed, and the engine started up.

Yes! Yes! Yes! Freedom!

I was too afraid to speak, so I waited for Ben to signal that all was well. I didn't have to wait long. The car came to a stop again and I heard Ben fiddle with the catch on the box. Then, daylight!

"Hey, gorgeous? Wanna go on a date?" Ben grinned.

"What do you think?" I answered. "But can I just take a bath first? I'm seriously over Eu De Basement by Mateo fucking Garcia."

"Sure, babe," Ben laughed and helped me out of the box.

"Peyton!" Mom yelled when I opened the car door. "Oh, my angel child."

"Hi, Mom," I said and hugged her tightly while she cried tears of joy.

"My sweetheart," Dad said and wrapped his arms around both of us.

"I'm so sorry," I said.

"Don't you dare," Dad insisted. "You did nothing to be sorry for."

We stood like that for a long time before Dad spoke to Ben.

"I don't know how to thank you, Ben."

"No thanks needed, Frank. I'm as elated as you are to have Peyton back safely."

"Are you hungry, baby?" Mom asked and looked me over. "Are you hurt?"

"I'm okay, Mom. I'd love to have a bath, though."

I couldn't wait to wash the remnants of Mateo and his basement off me.

"Of course, my child. You go soak in the tub and I'll make us something to eat," Mom cooed.

"I'll see you in a bit," Ben said.

It was so sweet of him to stay downstairs while I went for a bath. I thought it was very respectful of him toward my parents. What a gentleman he was.

"Okay."

I felt like Queen Cleopatra as I soaked away in a tub of warm, fragrant bath oil-infused water. I couldn't believe that something so simple could make me so happy. My mind kept wandering back to the basement. I couldn't stop the flashes from intruding on my peace.

I supposed I had been through a near-death experience, so coming out of it unscathed was a bridge too far. But I had every intention of putting the nightmare of Mateo behind me. All I wanted to focus on was my life with Ben.

There was a gentle knock at the door before it opened.

"Hey."

"Alyssa. Boy, are you a sight for sore eyes. Come in."

"How are you feeling, Pey?"

"Like I survived an avalanche."

"Worse. At least an avalanche is quick."

"True dat."

Alyssa sat down on the edge of the tub. I could see she'd been crying. I took her hand.

"It's okay, Lyssa. I'm okay."

"Fucking asshole," she muttered through her tears.

"Thanks to Ben, Mateo's reign of terror is finally over."

"The man is a saint, Peyton. If you don't snatch him up, I bloody well will."

I laughed as she wiped away her tears and sported her goofy grin.

"Oh, make no mistake. I'm never letting go of that man."

"Good for you."

"Was it awful, my friend? Did Mateo…you know…"

"No, thank God. He didn't touch me. Not that way, anyway. He got off on slapping me around, though."

"Do you think they'll trace his death back to you and Ben?"

"I'd be mightily impressed if they manage to find him. Mateo, like his two first wives, will forever be missing."

"As it should be."

"I'm going to go downstairs and help your mom in the kitchen. Take your time, but don't fall asleep in there. Okay?"

"Yeah, yeah. I'll be down soon."

Alyssa left the bathroom, and I cleaned up. Once I'd changed into clean clothes, I lay down on the bed for a minute to catch my breath.

"Hey, beautiful," Ben said and touched my arm.

It was dark in the room.

"What time is it?" I asked, confused.

"It's almost midnight. I was missing you."

"What?"

I must have fallen asleep after the bath.

"Are you hungry, my love?" Ben asked and kissed me on the forehead.

"Where is everyone?"

"They're all asleep. We didn't want to disturb you, so we had dinner without you. We figured you needed the rest more."

"I'm starving," I said.

Ben stood up but I caught him by the wrist.

"Not for food. For you. Come here."

27

BEN

Making love to Peyton was my ultimate dream. I loved her completely. I fell asleep with the love of my life resting in my arms, and I could have died happily, knowing that she was safe.

We spent two days with her family, after which Peyton was ready to return to New York with me.

"I was a little worried," I confessed to her on the flight back.

"Worried?"

"Yeah. Now that Mateo is no longer an issue, I thought that perhaps you'd want to move back to your hometown."

"And leave behind the man I love? Are you nuts?" she smiled.

"Well, you haven't said it in so many words, you know."

"I know, and I'm sorry about that."

"Don't apologize, my love. I think I understand why you were so guarded before. Having seen Mateo in the flesh, I get it."

"I never want either of us to say his name again, Ben. Never again."

"I agree."

Peyton and I spent the weekend squirreled away at home, making love and counting our blessings. It was bliss.

Although both of us had agreed to never say his name again, we kept an eye on the news, just in case there were any reports of Mateo's disappearance. The dirty cops were probably making a concerted effort to find their cash cow, but they were clearly careful not to make too much noise.

"I have an idea," I said on Sunday evening.

"Oh, yeah? Do tell."

"I think we should go to the cabin for a few days. We could use the distraction. What do you say?"

"It's a wonderful idea, Ben, but if I don't get back to work soon, the hospital will fire me."

"Don't you worry about that. I'll pull a few strings. The CEO owes me a favor. Would you like to go?"

"Are you kidding? Of course."

"Great. You get packing. I'll ask a colleague to locum for me so that my patients are taken care of."

"Sounds heavenly, Ben. Thank you."

"I love you, Peyton."

"I love you more, Ben."

* * *

"It's wonderful here, Ben," Peyton purred as we lay by the fireplace in the cabin.

"No argument here," I agreed and kissed her on the top of her head while she lay back against my chest.

"This feels so different from the last time."

"Different?"

"Yeah. I'm much more relaxed."

"I'm not surprised. No feelings of dread looming over you this time around."

"Indeed. So…what did you have in mind for the few days we're here?"

"We can do whatever you want, my beautiful."

"Hmmm…how much firewood did you say we had?"

"Enough to last two winters."

"Oh, good," Peyton grinned and pulled her sweater over her head and threw it down on the rug.

"I'm really starting to see why you like this cabin," I smiled.

"Prepare yourself for a whole lot of liking, Ben," she teased and unzipped my pants.

* * *

My family was none the wiser when it came to the ordeal that Peyton and I had been through. Owen had called me while I was in Mexico, but obviously, I couldn't tell him what I was up to, so I called him once we were back in the city.

"Hey, brother. You've been very quiet. Is everything alright?" he asked.

"I'm sorry, bro. Had to take care of something. It's all sorted now."

"Good. Wanna meet for a drink?" he suggested.

"Sure. Tonight, at the club?"

"Sounds good."

I called Peyton after work and told her I was meeting my brother at the club for a drink. She was getting ready to work the night shift.

"Enjoy, my love," she said. "I'll see you later."

"I'm proud of you, Pey."

"Why? What did I do?"

"You're the bravest woman I know."

"Couldn't have done it without you, babe."

Owen was waiting for me at the club when I arrived. He'd ordered me a beer.

"Well, if it isn't the jet setter," he smiled when I sat down. "I thought you said you were done with all this traipsing around the globe."

"Oh, trust me, I am. Thanks for the beer."

"Sure thing. So, what's news?"

I was bursting to tell someone about what had happened. Rowan was in Europe, plus I didn't want him to worry about me, so I guess that left my brother. I was nervous about telling him because I knew he'd crap all over me for not telling him beforehand. But I had to let it out, especially after Peyton and I agreed not to bring Mateo up in conversation again.

"I'm going to tell you something, Owen, but you have to swear to me that it will never leave this room. Okay?"

"Jeez, Ben. Sounds serious. Should I be concerned about you?" he asked me with a look of dread.

"No. No need to worry. It's all good. Just promise me."

"Fine. I promise. What's going on?"

"I was on my way to Mexico when you called me."

"Mexico? Why?"

"It's a crazy story, Owen. You just couldn't make this shit up if you tried."

"Okay…"

"Remember I told you that Peyton's ex knocked her around?"

"I remember."

"Well, there's much more to it than that, bro."

"How much more?"

"A fully ladened pantechnicon more. But, before I tell you, I want you to know that Peyton is innocent in all of this. She's the victim…was the victim."

"Just tell me, Ben."

"She was married until about a week and a half ago."

"Married! You're kidding."

"Yeah, to a man that makes Vlad the Impaler look like a cub scout. I tell you, Owen, you'd be lucky if you never met a human being like this in ten lifetimes."

"How did you find out about him?"

"Peyton told me. It's a long story, but I followed her one night after work because she'd been so damn secretive about everything. I'm not proud of it, but I had to find out more about her."

"Understandable."

"Anyway, she thought it was her husband following her, so she raced off and ended up colliding with a tree."

"Fuck! Is she okay?"

"Yeah, she's fine. That's when she told me the whole story. She ran away from him and was hiding out here in New York. He was the one who threw her down the stairs, causing her to lose her baby."

"Fucking hell, Ben. This is shocking."

"Yeah, but that's only the tip of the iceberg. It turns out this bastard had killed his first two wives and Peyton happened to find out about it. He tried to kill her too, and that's when she escaped and ran."

Owen pulled his hands through his hair. He stared at me incredulously.

"Fuck, Ben. You have to go to the cops. What if he comes after you?"

"I'm getting there."

"What the hell, bro? Why haven't you told me about this sooner? I would have been there with you."

"I didn't want to tell anyone, Owen. Turns out the guy had the Mexican cops in his back pocket. He was untouchable."

"Was?"

"Yeah. Let's just say he's not a problem anymore."

"What the hell are you talking about, Ben?"

I proceeded to tell my brother everything that had happened up to and including the death of Mateo. He just sat there, staring at me as if I'd gone mad. I knew he'd never tell a soul, but I felt as if I were betraying Peyton just by talking about the surreal ordeal.

When I was done, Owen called the waiter over and ordered two whiskeys—neat.

"I'm bloody furious with you, Ben. You know that right?"

"I know. I'm sorry, Owen, but I couldn't involve anyone else. Especially not my baby brother. I love you too much to see you hurt."

"So, now what?"

"Well, we've been keeping an eye on the news, but so far there hasn't been any mention of his disappearance."

"I take it they're not going to find any evidence?"

"Hell no. Sam took care of that. I didn't ask too many questions. Not that he would share the details with me in any case."

"Poor Peyton. How is she doing?"

"She's the bravest woman I've ever met. She's going to be just fine."

"I'm glad you told me, Ben. How are you doing? It can't be easy carrying this baggage around with you."

"Why do you think I told you? I had to get it out. I feel much better now. Sorry for dumping it on you."

"Don't be ridiculous. I know," he said after a few moments of silence between us, "There's no problem that a decent fishing trip can't sort out," he smiled. "What do you say we pack up the girls and a few cases of beer and hit the river for a weekend of nothing but fishing and open-flame dining?"

"You know what, little brother? That sounds like a damn fine idea."

"Great. Besides, you need to brush up on your fishing skills anyway. The last time I tallied the catches, you were left wanting, big bro."

"Oh, please. You're terrible at math. And you cheat!"

"Hey, I can't help it if I'm the family's fish whisperer," he grinned and ordered another round of beer.

I felt as if a weight had been lifted off my shoulders when I drove home that night. I never told Peyton about it, but I had nightmares for a long time after, during which I wrestled with Mateo for the knife. Suffice it to say that the fight didn't always end in my favor.

I wondered if I'd ever be the same again. I doubted it. Plunging a knife into another man's chest and watching him die changed the way one saw the world.

Sure, I'd killed before when I was in the military, but that was war.

You were in a war, Ben. It was either you and Peyton or Mateo. Don't give yourself such a hard time. It was an act of true love. Peyton needed you and there was no other option.

I kept telling myself that whenever I woke up in a cold sweat from the recurring nightmare. A few months after the incident, the dreams stopped. I was finally ready to get on with my life with Peyton.

28

PEYTON

I'd never told a soul, but every day after I'd lost my baby, I'd think about her. I wondered what she would have looked like, what her voice would have sounded like…things a mother dreams of before she meets her child. I tried to forget that she had ever existed, but it was impossible.

A year had passed since Mateo's death. My life was on track again. I was loving every minute at the hospital, and I cherished my time with Ben. But something was missing. I knew the void would always be there. I wanted a child.

I chose to talk to Ben about it one night after we'd made love. He must have sensed that I had something on my mind. He was very intuitive when it came to me.

"What's the matter, my love?" he asked. "Aren't you happy?"

"Of course. I'm very happy, darling. It's just…"

"What? You know you can tell me anything."

"Everything about our life together is perfect, Ben. Our careers make us happy; we have amazing friends, and our families are incredible. But I feel like something is missing. I want a baby."

There. I'd said it.

"Okay…"

"What's wrong? Don't you? Aren't you ready?"

"My love. Of course, I'm ready. I can't imagine anything more exciting than sharing a child with you."

"Then why the hesitance?"

"Well, I'm not sure if it's going to be smooth sailing. The pregnancy, I mean. There was a lot of damage done when…when you fell down the stairs and lost your first child, my love."

"I know. But, Ben, you are the most talented surgeon in your field. You can fix it, can't you?"

"Of course, I'll try my best, Peyton. But I don't want you to get your hopes up. I don't want to be responsible for not being able to give you your dream. Our dream."

I realized that I was putting a lot of pressure on Ben. I felt remorse about that. But honestly, I knew that if anyone could help me, it was him.

"Please, try."

"Okay, my love. I can't say no to you. I'll try my best. But promise me you won't put too much pressure on your body to do this. I love you so much, even if we can't have children. I'll always love you, Pey."

"I won't. Thank you, babe."

I snuggled in his arms, satisfied that he wouldn't let me down.

"The good news is that we'll get to have plenty of baby-making sex if you're successful," I purred and kissed the place of his arm when Mateo had slashed into the flesh.

The scar had all but healed, but I had a feeling the traces would remain as a reminder of how close I'd come to losing my Ben.

Madison called me the next day.

"Hey, sis. How are you? How's little Gabi?"

"Hi, Pey. We're all great, thanks. Craig and I decided that he needs to go for the snip. Honestly, I think my heart was a few sizes too big when I thought that having more than three kids would be fun. Gabi had cured me of that dumb ass idea."

I laughed.

"That busy, is she?"

"OMG, Pey. She's got more spunk than the two boys put together. The kid is allergic to sitting still. We went to the beach the other day, and I swear I dug around in my bag for a mere ten seconds just to look up again and find Madam was missing."

"Oh, crap, Madi. What happened?"

"Her Highness took a stroll to see if she could find anything interesting to eat in someone else's bag. The kid scared the shit out of me. There I was, running around the beach like a mad woman, thinking my kid had been kidnapped."

"Shit, Madi. Where'd you find her?"

"The little shit was chatting away to the lifeguard and sharing his packet of crisps with him. Well, I was finished! We packed up and went home. I swear, I'm going to have to put a leash on that kid."

I couldn't help laughing at my sister. Madi had always been so calm and put together. Hearing her losing her shit was oddly comforting. I didn't feel like the inadequate baby sister anymore.

"Anyway, I didn't call to complain about my pint-sized terrorist. How are you and Ben? How's work?"

"Ben is an angel, and work is exhausting but good."

"That's wonderful, Pey. What else is news?"

"I spoke to Ben last night about having a baby."

"Oh, that's wonderful. What did he say?"

"He's keen. It's not going to be easy, though. I'm not sure I can fall pregnant after the mess Mateo made of me."

"I'm so sorry, Peyton. My heart aches for you."

"Thanks, Madi. Ben is going to see if he can do a little damage control. Pray for us."

"Of course. When is he going to operate?"

"I'll let you know."

We chatted for a while longer before we hung up.

Hope springs eternal, Peyton.

* * *

The pressure was on. The burden of helping Peyton and hopefully being instrumental in her being able to have a successful pregnancy weighed heavily on me. I called in a few experts in the field of surgical gynecology to assist me with the operation.

Peyton was nervous. I could tell by the way she was chewing away furiously on her button lip as she lay on the gurney in the operating theater.

"Stop stressing, my love. That's my job," I smiled and kissed her.

"Ugh! I wish it was over already."

"You and me both, beautiful. Are you ready?"

Peyton nodded.

Two theater nurses came over to her and helped her onto the operating table. They hooked her up to an IV, and soon we were all present and ready to rock and roll.

"Okay, pretty lady," the anesthetist smiled, "you know the drill. Let's start counting."

I listened as Peyton started at ten. She was out before she could get to six.

"Okay, gentlemen, and lady. Let's see what we can do here," I said, took the scalpel, and made an incision.

An hour and a half later, we sewed Peyton up and I went to the sink to take off the gloves and the apron. Both were covered in blood.

"That was tough, Ben, Dr. Andrews said and did the same."

"The toughest one yet," I agreed.

"You did a splendid job in there, Dr. Forbes," he said again.

"Thank you."

"I don't think anyone could have done more."

"I just hope it was enough."

"All we and the patient can do now is wait. It will take time to heal. I don't know about you, but I'm hopeful."

I waited with Peyton until she was awake.

"How did it go?" she asked, all groggy.

"It went well, my love. Now we wait."

"Okay," she said and closed her eyes again."

Please, God, Give this poor woman a chance at motherhood.

* * *

Alyssa was spending the week with me. I was on bed rest after the operation, so Ben called her and the two surprised me. It was wonderful having her with me. Especially since it hurt like hell just to pee!

Alyssa was an excellent nurse. Her cooking skills left much to be desired, but I wasn't that hungry anyway and Ben was great at bringing home dinner.

"I'm tired of talking about myself," I said. "Tell me about your life, Lyssa."

"Well, mine isn't half as exciting as yours, but I enjoy it," she said while she sat at the edge of the bed, painting her nails.

"Do you have your beady eye on any cute doctors?"

"Funny you should ask," she grinned.

"What? Have you been holding out on me?"

"No, but you've been a little distracted of late, so I thought I'd wait a while to brag."

"Spill it!" I pushed myself up on the pillow. "Ouch, damn it. This hurts."

"Here, let me help you."

"Your nails are wet. I'll manage."

"Ugh…okay, that's better. I'm all ears. Who is this lucky man?"

"His name is Tom. He's a fourth-year resident, specializing in plastic surgery. Not that he'll ever need any. The Lord made that man perfect!"

"Uh-oh, I know that look. You're in love, aren't you?"

"Desperately."

"Are the two of you doing the nasty?"

"Peyton Taylor! I'm a chaste and decent woman."

I couldn't help laughing...which hurt like a bitch!

"Oh, please, stop. Laughing hurts," I said and held onto my gut.

"Okay, okay. If you must know, yes. We have, and let me tell you, it's the best sex I've ever had! Bar none. But it's not just the sex. It's everything. I gotta tell you, Pey, I think he's the one."

"Whoa, slow down. This from a woman who used to scoff at marriage? Who are you?"

"Tom's amazing. I'll bring him along the next time I visit."

"Where's he from?"

"Texas."

"Yehaa, cowgirl," I grinned. "Saddle up."

Alyssa was glowing. I loved it.

"How are you really, Pey?"

"I'm happy. Ben is a dream come true. I just hope this operation turns out to be a success. I would love to have his babies."

"You're going to look back on this moment, one day when you're cursing at your kids for dragging mud through the house and laugh at how silly you were for doubting."

"From your lips to God's ears, Lyssa."

"Amen."

Ben came home early. He brought steak and grilled it outside on the open flame. It reminded me of the first time I visited his house. Who would have guessed back then how my life would pan out?

No Mateo, a budding career, a wonderful man who loved me passionately, and the hope of having a baby of my own.

Ben and I retired early for the night. I lay on his arm while we chatted in the dark.

"How was your day, beautiful?" Ben asked while he stroked my hair.

"It was good. Missing you though. I'm glad you were able to come home early."

"I've been so busy, I feel like I'm neglecting you."

"Nonsense. Besides, Alyssa is keeping well entertained. She's got a new man in her life."

"Oh?"

"Uh-huh. A doctor from Texas. Sounds like it's serious."

"Well, if he's from Texas, he must be used to roping and breaking in wild horses," Ben chuckled.

"He must be very skilled. As are you, my sexy sensei."

"Hhmm, you just earned yourself a delicate treat," Ben play-growled and disappeared beneath the sheets.

"Be careful," I gasped.

"Trust me. I'm a doctor."

29

PEYTON

"**I** know that nibble," Ben said one morning while I was staring at my body in the full-length mirror in the bedroom. "What's bothering you, babe?"

"It's been eight months, Ben. Eight months!"

There was no feeling more demoralizing to a woman than buying a pregnancy test each and every month, holding your breath during the allotted three minutes, and finding a negative result time and time again. I was utterly fed up.

"My love," Ben said and came over to put his arms around me. "Eight months isn't long, considering…"

"Considering I'm a hot mess," I ended his sentence.

"No, you're not," he said and gently rubbed his hand over my tummy. "You're beautiful…a little impatient…but beautiful. Besides, I must tell you. I'm *really* enjoying the practice," he purred and nuzzled my neck.

"I'm sorry, babe. I know I'm acting like a lunatic."

Ben turned me around so I could face him.

"Peyton, I'll have you any way I can. I love you."

I giggled and kissed him.

"I love you too, Ben."

"Now, get your cute ass into those scrubs, and let's go to work."

"Yes, Sensei Forbes."

I called Alyssa on my way to the hospital.

"Nyepp…What's up, Doc?" she answered.

"Funny. I'm down, I need a quick pep talk."

"Okay, let's see. You have a stunning ass, you're very smart…uhm… you live with the most perfect man to ever draw breath…"

"And still I can't fall pregnant," I interrupted.

"Ahhh, babe. Stop that. You're just hormonal. You'll get there. You have to be patient."

"I love you so much, Lyssa, but if you say that to me one more time, I'm going to have to end you."

"Yikes! Those fertility meds are making you seriously cranky. I hope you haven't done anything awful to Ben yet."

"No. How can I? He's perfect. I'm the broken one."

"Stop it, Pey. You're not broken. Just a little slow off the mark."

"Thanks, babe. Sorry for being a bummer."

"Okay, go prescribe some drugs. Always makes me feel better."

"Fine. Talk to you later."

Alyssa was right. My hormones were up and down like a seesaw. The days when I was dragging my ass in the dirt were the hardest. It was one of those days. I felt awful. Tired as hell, and rather moody.

Halfway through the day, I snuck off to find a quiet place where I could lie down my head for a few minutes.

"Peyton. Peyton, wake up."

I opened my eyes to find Olivia standing over me. I must have fallen asleep.

"You really need to tell Ben to let you get some rest at night," she grinned. "You've been asleep for two hours. I'm sorry to wake you, but if the supervisor finds you, she'll chew you out."

"Oh, crap," I said, wiping my eyes. "Thanks, Livvy. I owe you one."

"No sweat."

I sat up and rubbed my face.

"Are you sure you're not pregnant?" she asked me.

"I wish. It's the injections. They make me feel like I'm permanently hungover."

"Okay, if you say so. But I'd check if I were you."

"And waste another month's wages on pregnancy tests? Hell no."

"Fine, grumpy chops. I'll see you out there."

"Ugh! Thanks."

Could it be? Olivia did have a point. I hadn't taken a test in a while, and I was late. But I was often late, so.

The shift dragged on, and I couldn't wait to get home and sleep. I hit the pillow with a vengeance when I got home that night. I was fast asleep when Ben got home. I slept right through, in fact, until morning.

"Well, hello, Sleeping Beauty," he said and placed a cup of coffee next to me on the nightstand.

"Wow. I can't believe I slept right through. Sorry, babe."

"Don't be silly. You must have needed it. How are you feeling?"

"A little better, actually."

"Great. Here," he said and handed me a pregnancy test, "whizz on this for Doctor."

"Seriously, Ben?"

"Uh-huh. Humor me."

"Ugh…fine."

I took it and went to the toilet. I peed on the stick, left it on the edge of the tub, and went back to get my coffee.

"Did you change the brand? This coffee tastes funny."

Ben went to the bathroom and came back, holding the stick.

"Uhm, I think you may want to have a look at this," he said and smiled.

No! Could it be? Was I?

He handed it to me and there it was. Two lines!

I stared at the little window. I was speechless for a few moments.

"Congratulations, my love. You did it," Ben grinned and kissed me.

"No, you did it, Ben," I said and started crying.

"Those better be happy tears."

"Yeah," I sobbed, "I think so. Who the hell knows? I'm an emotional wreck."

"Welcome to motherhood, baby," he laughed and hugged me tightly.

* * *

Madi and Alyssa went nuts when I shared the news with them. Mom cried and Dad started buying balance bikes and padded baseball bats.

Ben's family was equally excited. Owen and Suzy were engaged and super excited for us. Ben's parents offered to start a college fund and brought over a giant-sized bear to congratulate us.

Ben and I were so happy. I was a bit nervous, though. It had been so difficult to conceive, I worried that we were getting all hyped up too soon. But Ben talked me up and insisted that I stay positive. God bless him.

"Are you ready, honey?" he asked me as he squirted the gel onto the ultrasound probe.

"Are you kidding? I've been ready for eight months!" I grinned.

I was about six weeks along and couldn't wait to see who was causing all the fuss inside my body.

Ben watched the ultrasound monitor as he moved the probe around. I was too nervous to look, so I stared at the ceiling.

"And?" I asked impatiently.

"Take a look."

I took a deep breath before I turned to look.

"What? Am I seeing this right?" I asked, very slowly.

"That depends. What are you seeing?"

"Either our baby has three legs, or…"

"Or there are two babies in there," Ben grinned, proud as punch.

"What? Twins!"

"No wonder you're so tired all the time. Your body is working hard."

"Holy…are they okay?"

"Now, what kind of a question is that? They're our babies. Of course, they're okay. Strong like bulls."

"Can you see the sex?"

"I'm looking. Give me a second."

Two babies! Wow! I couldn't believe it. I was shooting for one, but, hey…two would do nicely, too.

"Can you tell, babe?" I asked impatiently.

"I can only tell that one of them is a boy. The other baby is hiding its gender. I'm sure we'll be able to tell at a later stage."

"No. I don't want to know," I said on impulse. "Let's keep it a surprise."

"Uhm, that might be a problem for me. I'll be doing the scans. I'll have to see."

"That's fine. But don't tell me. Okay?"

"Okay, you crazy girl," Ben grinned.

"Hey, crazy as a fox," I smiled.

"I love you, you nutter," Ben laughed and kissed me.

"Oi, it's already full in there. Don't get any ideas," I teased.

"Honey, there's always room for Daddy."

I felt like a whale. My boobs hurt, my ankles were getting fat, and I'd never peed so much in my life! But, I was deliriously happy. I was seven months along and Alyssa was visiting me for a few days.

We were at a coffee shop, where I'd gotten into the habit of ordering a watermelon and feta salad, with added anchovies. It was pretty standard, and the waitress brought it to me without me even asking.

"You're a whack job, Pey," Alyssa said as she watched me scoffing.

"Wait until you get weird cravings. I can't help it. This tastes sooo good."

Alyssa laughed and ate her bacon and eggs.

"Ugh! I have to pee again. I'll be right back."

"Uh-huh."

I waddled across to the bathroom and sat down to pee for arguably the twentieth time that morning. That was when I saw it. My body went cold.

No! Blood.

"What's wrong, Pey?" Alyssa asked when I returned to the table, "You're pale as a ghost."

"I'm bleeding," was all I could say.

Alyssa took a moment before she registered.

"Uhm, okay. Don't panic. Let's get you to Ben. I'll pay the bill."

My head was spinning. I couldn't think. It was as if my mind had executed a shutdown without my permission.

"Okay," was all I could utter.

* * *

"Talk to me, Ben," I pleaded while he looked at the monitor.

"It's okay, Peyton. Calm down, my love. The babies are fine."

"Are you sure? Why the hell am I bleeding?"

"It's placenta previa, darling. You're bleeding quite a bit, so you'll have to spend the rest of your pregnancy in bed, but the babies will be fine."

"Oh, thank God. I was so scared, Ben."

"Well, if it's any consolation, I think I need to change your underwear," he said and let out a deep breath.

"I'm sorry, babe."

"You have nothing to be sorry for. You're doing great."

"Bedrest? Really?"

"Uh-huh. I know it's a bummer, but it's the safest option."

"You'd better let Alyssa in. She must be frantic out there in the waiting room."

* * *

"Hey, sis. How are you feeling?"

"Climbing the walls. I tell you, Madi, if I don't see a bed for another year it will be too soon."

"Huh! You say that now. Wait until the babies are born. You know what they say about twins—twice the fun, four times the work."

"Anything has to be better than watching reruns of Dallas and Friends."

"All I'm saying is be careful what you wish for."

"I guess."

"By the way. I spoke to Mom and Craig, and they've agreed to watch the clan so I can be with you when you give birth."

"Oh, Madi! That's wonderful news."

"Isn't it? I get to see your new babies and I get to finish a sentence and pee without being interrupted," she laughed.

"When are you coming?"

"You're having the C-section next week, aren't you?"

"Yes, and not a moment too soon, I'll have you know."

"Great. I'll see you in a few days, then. I'm so proud of you, Pey."

"What? For finally getting knocked up?" I teased.

"Yes, that. And for keeping the faith."

"Thank you, Madi. I love you."

* * *

"Hello, again," the theater nurse greeted me with a smile.

"Yup, I'm back," I grinned, nervously.

"This is a very exciting day for you and Dr. Forbes," she smiled. "We couldn't be happier."

"Thank you."

"Hey, beautiful," Ben's voice echoed in the passage. "Ready to meet our babies?"

"Are you kidding? I've been ready all my life."

"You're so cute," he smiled and kissed me. "Okay. Let's get us some babies, baby."

"I'm ready."

The epidural wasn't painful, just uncomfortable. Soon afterward I felt nothing from the waist down. I couldn't see past the screen, but I listened to the chatter. I felt tugging and saw a nurse carrying a little bundle to the corner of the room.

"Is the baby, okay?" I asked, nervously.

A tiny little voice started wailing.

"Oh, yes. Your son has a fine pair of lungs."

A few moments later, another little bundle made its appearance.

"Ben? What is it?"

Another, tinier voice, started up a racket.

"Ben?"

"It's alright, my love. We have them both. They're beautiful."

I heard one of the surgeons say that he would stitch me up. Ben came around the screen and held our newborns in his arms.

"Congratulations, beautiful. We have ourselves a pigeon pair."

30

PEYTON

"I'll go," Ben said and placed his hand on my back.

The twins were beautiful, but, boy, did Madi hit the nail on the head. My life was an endless array of milk-spotted bras and shirts, throw up on my shoulders, midnight feeds, and nappy patrols.

Ben was brilliant. Once the initial few days were done and Madi went back home to tend to her three children, he jumped in and helped wherever he could. There was no way I could go back to work for the time being, but I didn't mind. There'd be plenty of time to be a doctor. I threw myself, boots and all, into motherhood.

Saturdays were our 'family outing' days. The babies were three months old, and Ben and I took them along to breakfast at a deli near our home. Ben bought one of those twin strollers that looked like it could be used for serious off-roading, and we took turns pushing the gang around the hood.

The waitress who had previously delivered the watermelon concoction now knew to bring me a full English breakfast and a gallon of decaf coffee. Ben stuck to the continental breakfast option and smiled whenever he watched me inhaling my food.

"Hey, I'm breastfeeding," I'd grin.

"I long for the days when those perfectly perky puppies used to be all mine," he winked.

"So do I."

"I thought we could have the family over for a barbeque this Sunday," he said and took a sip of his coffee.

"That will be nice."

"Great."

Leyla made a fuss, so Ben picked her up and distracted her. She adored her daddy. Chad was fast asleep. He loved his sleep. Not that I was complaining.

"She's a feisty one. Just like her mommy," Ben teased.

"It seems that the women in my family are built that way."

We finished our meal and took a stroll back home. I had a quick nap while Ben and the babies watched a game of football on TV. My life was bliss.

Sunday morning came around quickly. Then again, time flew when you were the mother of twin babies. The doorbell rang and Ben went to answer.

"Your folks are a little early, aren't they?" I said and looked at my watch.

"Hello!" I heard from the entrance hall. "Where's my princess?"

"Dad?"

Mom and Dad came strolling into the living room as if it was no big thing.

"What are you guys doing here?" I said excitedly.

"I heard there was a barbecue, and you know how I feel about ribeye," Dad chuckled and gave me a big hug.

"Surprise," Mom smiled.

"What? Ben? Did you do this?"

"Of course. I did promise you a family barbecue."

"Oh, you sneak. Thank you, babe."

"You're welcome, sweetheart."

"Where are my grandbabies?" Dad insisted.

"Yes, we've been dying to see them again. I know it's only been two months, but I'll bet they're twice the size they were the last time."

"I'll get them."

I looked back and saw my dad and Ben chatting happily. My heart was overflowing with gratitude and love.

* * *

"Peyton looks so happy, Ben. I know she's happy to be a mom, but I know you have made the biggest contribution to her joy. Thank you, Ben."

"I love your daughter so much. She's made me happier than I ever thought I could be. And the twins are a joy. Can we take a walk in the garden, Frank? There's something I wanted to talk to you about."

"Sure. Is everything okay?"

"Oh, yeah. There's no problem."

Frank and I left the room while the women cooed over the twins. I was a little nervous.

"I wanted to ask you something, Frank."

"Go ahead."

"I want to marry Peyton and I would like your blessing."

"I see."

"I know we did things a little backward, but I think the time is right now for us to make it official."

"Ben, you are a treasure. Nothing would make me happier, Son."

Frank shook my hand and then pulled me in for a bear hug.

"Welcome to the family," he said.

"Glad to be a part of it, Dad."

My folks, Owen, and Suzy arrived just after noon. The music was playing outside at the pool and the women were chatting away, faffing with the kids. It was picture-perfect.

I stood up at the luncheon table and tapped my glass. All eyes turned to me.

"I can't tell you how wonderful it is to have you all here," I started. "Frank, Millie, thank you for making time to be here with us. As for the Forbes clan, try and leave some food for our guests, okay?"

"Who gave this clown permission to speak," Owen heckled, and dished another piece of ribeye onto his plate.

"Alright, settle down," I laughed and then turned to Peyton.

"Peyton, love of my life, thank you for making this day special. I love you with all my heart and I have another gift for you."

I reached into my pocket and pulled out a box. I heard gasps around the table as I opened it up and held it in front of her.

"Peyton Taylor, will you make me the happiest man in the universe and marry me?"

251

She looked at me with big eyes and then back at the ring.

"Uhm, I think you meant to say, Doctor Peyton Taylor," she smirked, sporting great big teary eyes. "And yes. I will marry you, Sensei Forbes."

* * *

"Why am I so nervous?" I said, trying to button up my bodice with shaky fingers.

"You're supposed to be," Alyssa laughed. "You're about to become 'the wife', 'the ball and chain', the…"

"Serves me right for asking a stupid question," I said and rolled my eyes. "Help me with this damn button, will you?"

"You look stunning, Pey," she said and helped me with the pesky button.

"You do, and Ben couldn't ask for a more perfect bride," Madi added.

"Thank you, guys."

"Hi, precious," Mom said as she came into the room. "Wow. You look so beautiful, sweetheart."

Mom had been watching the twins while I got dressed. This was my second wedding, but, honestly, as far as I was concerned it was the first and only one that mattered.

Ben and I had been together long enough for me to know exactly who he was. I had absolutely no doubts that I was marrying the man of my dreams—the father of my children and my soulmate.

"Ben is going to impregnate you with another set of twins when he sees you in this dress," Alyssa grinned.

"Please, no. One set is enough. I think I'll be happy with just one next time."

"Next time? And to think I was considered the breeder of the family," Madison laughed.

"Looks like you've got yourself some healthy sibling rivalry going on here, Madi," Alyssa said and slapped me on the butt.

"Oh, no. You're next, Dr. Collins. In fact, I'm rather shocked to see that you haven't snagged that Texan of yours yet. You're slipping, Lyssa."

"All in good time. I'm working on it," she smiled.

"He is rather yummy, Alyssa," Madi added.

"Isn't he just?" Mom weighed it.

"Okay, you lot. Back off. I saw him first," she laughed.

"How are we doing for time?" I asked, making sure all the buttons were done up.

"Another twenty minutes, darling," Mom answered.

"Are the twins, okay?" I asked, feeling guilty for having seemingly abandoned my children.

"They're fine. Your Dad took them for a walk. He took the padded baseball bat and a ball with him, so I'm sure they're enjoying a waddle across the lawn."

"Oh, crap. I hope he doesn't bring them back all covered in mud."

"Don't worry, Pey. I brought a full tub of wet wipes along, just in case."

"How's my almost daughter-in-law?" Frances asked as she came into the room, carrying my bouquet. "Oh, my! Peyton, sweety, you look like a princess."

"Thank you," I smiled.

Ben's parents had made me feel like I was family long before he asked me to marry him. They were wonderful with the twins and spoiled them rotten.

"Ben is chomping at the bit," she whispered. "I've never seen him so nervous."

"Oh, good. So, it's not just me," I laughed.

There was a faint knock on the door. It was Alan.

"Is the bride ready?" he called through the door. "I think we'd better get this show on the road before the groom grows any paler."

"We're ready, darling," Frances laughed. "Five minutes."

"Is Dad back yet?"

"I'm here, princess," I heard my dad's voice on the other side of the door.

"Alright, hens, let's go," Mom said.

I was left alone for a moment. I looked, one more time, at my reflection in the mirror.

"You look stunning, my beautiful daughter," Dad smiled. "Come, let's walk down that aisle. I'm here. You can lean on my arm, sweetheart."

"Second time's the charm, hey, Dad?"

"You bet."

* * *

Peyton was a stunning bride. My heart dropped to my feet when I watched her walking toward me down the aisle. The 'I am' couldn't come soon enough for me.

After the ceremony and the reception, and after we'd fished the rice out of our clothes, I took my bride away for a few days of solitude.

My folks were more than happy to have the twins over while Peyton and I were on honeymoon. I had one more surprise in store for my perfect wife. We were lying in front of a roaring fire in the cabin that had become our love nest of choice.

We'd spent the day skiing the slopes and enjoying a meal at the restaurant we'd discovered. I opened a bottle of wine, the same vintage we'd shared the first time we stayed over at the cabin, and we were just snuggling in the glow of the amber flames.

"This is perfect, isn't it?" Peyton sighed. "I'm so glad you brought us here for our honeymoon, babe."

"I'm glad you feel that way, beautiful."

"Oh, I do. This is as close to paradise as I'll ever be. I wish we could stay here all the time."

"What? And miss out on the noise and the pollution of the city? Have you lost your mind, Mrs. Forbes?"

"Yeah, yeah. City life is good for business, I suppose. But you can't blame a girl for dreaming."

"I have a little gift for you, my beautiful wife," I purred and kissed her naked shoulder.

"Oh? Careful, dear. You're going to spoil me."

"Is that a bad thing?"

"Hell, no. What did you get me?" she grinned.

"Wait here. I'll fetch it."

Peyton let rip and belted out quite a wolf whistle as I strolled across the living room in the buff.

"Why, thank you, Ma'am."

"If the gift is that sweet ass of yours, it's perfect," she giggled.

"Honey, you can sink your nails into that anytime you like."

"Damn right, Sensei."

I returned to the fireplace holding a small box.

"Here you go, Mrs. Forbes," I said and handed it to her.

"Ooh, how exciting," Peyton said and opened the box.

Inside was a key. She took it out and held it up.

"Okay, I don't get it. Is this a key to our home? You do know I've been living there for a while now."

"Duhh. No, silly. It's the key to your new home."

"New home? Where?"

"This home. I bought it for you."

"What? Are you messing with me Ben Forbes?"

"Would I? It's yours, baby."

"Ben! I...I don't know what to say."

"I'll settle for 'actions speak louder than words', sexy."

"Ben, I'm going to *actions* your brains out!"

31

EXCERPT: MY BEST FRIEND'S DAD

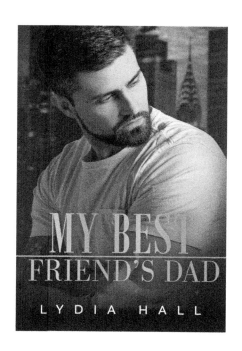

Acrush on my best friend's dad cost me my most precious years in college.

I couldn't even consider another guy. I was *obsessed* with Edward.

Twenty years older, and a ruthless businessman.

Those things should *not* make it to the list of qualities I want in a man.

And yet, here I am, drooling over him right after I accepted his job offer.

So now, on top of everything else, he's also my boss.

Edward's touch sets me on fire, but it would only have to last in the moment.

His arms might be my safe haven, but a future with him is impossible.

I truly believe that, but the positive pregnancy test tells a different story.

It paints an uncertain future that I'd never expected.

The news would destroy every relationship, and my head tells me to run away.

Will he come looking for me if I do?

Maddie

"Madelyne Williams," Mrs. Davies, my seventh-grade teacher, called.

I stood up, smoothed out the creases on my blouse and pleated skirt, and walked to the center of the room, where almost a hundred pairs of eyes watched me closely.

My whole seventh grade class, along with many of their parents, had gathered to view the end of term presentations.

Mrs. Davies had called me to go first.

I'd been preparing my presentation on Martin Luther King Junior, and the 1950's civil rights movement, for months, knowing whatever grade we get on the presentations would go to our final overall grade at the end of the year.

With a grade average of High A's, I had a reputation to maintain.

Before I started to give my presentation, I scanned the group of gathered adults, looking out for my mother and father.

They'd promised me they'd be here.

I quickly caught sight of my governess, Mrs. Yorke, and sighed.

Of course, my parents weren't here. They were never here. Why should I expect anything different?

It didn't matter that they'd promised they'd be here. It wasn't the first promise to me my parents had broken. For a family to whom appearances meant everything it seemed only their appearances were important. As long as I was safely tucked away at Boston's top private school, and maintaining my excellent grades, in my parents' eyes their job had successfully been done.

I swallowed around the hurt and frustration bubbling in my throat, plastered my best smile on my face, and began giving my presentation.

By the end of it, Mrs. Davies was beaming, and all the parents were clapping. I saw Mrs. Yorke grinning with pride, as she clapped the loudest of all.

"Excellent work, Madelyne. I have no doubt you'll be maintaining your excellent grade record," Mrs. Davies said, as I pushed a lock of long, red hair behind my ear, and returned to my desk.

The rest of the class's presentations followed, and I listened intently like an obedient student, as we heard submissions on various topics, like Newton's laws of motion, the Scientific Revolution and Little Women, by Louisa May Alcott.

All the parents applauded after every presentation, and Mrs. Davies found something to compliment in every submission. In fact, a few of my classmates had really stepped up their game, giving presentations on par with my own. It felt great to be challenged academically.

Once all the presentations had been given, Mrs. Davies allowed us a few moments to chat with our parents, and I walked over to Mrs. Yorke.

"Brilliant work, Maddie," she complimented, reaching out to squeeze my hand. "Your parents send their love, and their apologies that they couldn't be here. Your father had a last minute, unexpected meeting with the mayor."

My father's work as a politician always came first, and my mother was never not by his side.

I knew I should have been grateful. My father's work meant that we lived in luxury in the Beacon Hill neighborhood, and I attended the best private school in the city.

But still…

I pushed the thoughts aside, plastered a smile on my face and said, "Thank you. And thank you for coming to see my presentation."

"I wouldn't be anywhere else, sweetheart," Mrs. Yorke insisted, squeezing my hand again.

Out of all the governesses and nannies I'd had over the years, Mrs. Yorke was by far my favorite. She was an older woman, in her mid-sixties, with a distinct grandmotherly demeanor about her. Even though she always acted in a professional manner and held me at a slight distance like the other governesses had, but over the three years she'd been my father's employee, Mrs. Yorke and I had grown quite close.

After the parents left the assembly hall, Mrs. Davies led us back to our classroom. I settled at my desk and got out my math book in preparation for the next lesson.

"No need for books today," Mrs. Davies said, addressing the whole class.

I sighed and slipped my book back in my satchel, disappointed we wouldn't be having a math lesson. It was one of my favorite subjects.

"I have something much more exciting for you than algebra," she said, gesturing to the front row where a girl with long, curly brown hair sat. I didn't recognize her as one of my classmates and watched with interest as Mrs. Davies beckoned her forwards.

"This is Shannon Jackson. She and her father just moved here, and she'll be joining the class."

Shannon smiled shyly. She was about my height -- which was above average for other thirteen-year-olds -- and she had a sporty physique. Her skin was sun kissed and dotted with freckles, making me think she spent a lot of time outside. But the thing that really drew me to Shannon was her warm, hazel eyes.

I gave her a welcoming smile, which she returned with a grin.

Mrs. Davies' gaze flitted between Shannon and I, and she smiled. "Madelyne, I'd like you to help Shannon get settled in here. Show her around the school, and how we do things at Benjamin Franklin Academy. I'm sure you'll be friends in no time."

"It would be my pleasure, Mrs. Davies," I replied politely.

"And, as a reward for everyone's hard work, I think we should have an extended recess. Everyone make their way outside, while I speak to the school kitchen staff to arrange a special treat for everyone."

The teaching assistant, Miss. Addams led us all outside, while Mrs. Davies made her way to the kitchen.

It was nearing the end of the fall term, and the weather in Boston had turned cold, so I was glad of my thick, sheepskin lined coat, and woolen gloves and hat, as we all stepped outside.

The boys in class quickly warmed themselves up when they saw Coach Phillips on the football field and started up an impromptu game.

I found Shannon by the edge of the field, watching intently.

"Hey, I'm Maddie," I said, drawing the other girl's attention to me.

Shannon turned, a brilliant smile on her face, and said, "Great to meet you, Maddie. I heard your presentation. It really was the best in the class."

"Thank you."

Shannon's attention drifted back to the field for a moment, and she asked, "So, is there a girls' team?"

I sighed. "Sadly, no. Apparently, football isn't an appropriate sport for young ladies."

We both rolled our eyes. "We're stuck with gymnastics. Not that I'm much of an athlete."

"In my old school, I was captain of the girl's football team. I guess I could try out for gymnastics though," Shannon said.

She didn't sound convinced, and trying to change the subject, I asked, "So, where did you move here from?"

"Up until recently, I lived at the military base in Taunton," Shannon said, and I caught the tone of discomfort in her voice.

Had her father been discharged from the military for some misdemeanor? I wondered.

Before I could ask any more questions, Shannon quickly redirected the conversation. "So, who is the hot quarterback?"

Her eyes drifted back to the field, as she watched the boys play their game.

"That's Tyler Mitchell, captain of the team."

"Is he single?" Shannon asked, watching as Tyler sprinted across to Coach Phillips to ask him something.

"He is," I confirmed, my gaze focusing on Coach Phillips. The thing I wasn't about to tell Shannon was I'd much rather watch Coach Phillips than any of the boys on the team.

Boys my own age drove me insane. It wasn't just their immature sense of humor, and how none of them seemed to have much direction in life. Well, apart from Tyler, who was convinced he was going to play for The New England Patriots. I understood that at thirteen, no one was thinking about settling down, getting married or having kids, but all the guys in my grade treated girls like they were an expendable commodity. Tyler had a reputation of moving from one girl to the next, never sticking with anyone for more than a few weeks.

"Though I wouldn't hold your breath. He isn't the commitment type."

Shannon laughed, her eyes still not leaving Tyler. "Neither am I. But if he needs a date for the Christmas party, I won't say no. Neither would I turn down a goodnight kiss. Who are you going to the party with?"

"No one," I answered honestly. It wasn't just because I found guys my age immature. Even if I had wanted to date anyone in our grade, there's no way my parents would let me. My father had given strict orders that I wasn't allowed to date until I was at least eighteen.

"Oh, well, dates are overrated anyway. We'll go to the party together," Shannon said, linking her arm through mine and turning away from the football field.

We crossed the school yard, and I was surprised to feel that the ache in my heart caused by my parents' absence earlier was fading much more quickly than usual.

Even though I was used to them disappointing me, it always stung when they broke their promises. But for once the sting wasn't quite so bitter because for the first time in years, I wasn't alone.

"Do you want to come to mine after school?" Shannon asked, as we found a bench out of the wind to settle on. "I was never allowed people over when we lived on the military base, but now Dad's left the military, I'm sure he won't mind."

The only person expecting me that afternoon was Mrs. Yorke, and I knew she wouldn't mind if I went to Shannon's house. Either way, she'd get paid.

"I'd love to. Thanks. I'll need to call my governess to let her know not to pick me up."

"Don't your mom or dad pick you up?" Shannon asked.

"Unlikely. Dad's on the campaign trail. He's probably still cozying up to Mayor Daniels. And Mom will be with him for support."

"I'm sorry," Shannon said, with genuine sympathy in her tone. "I know what it's like not having your parents around much. Until recently, I hardly ever saw my dad. Since he left the military, he's trying to make it up to me."

Shannon didn't say why her dad had left the military, or where her mom was, and even though I was curious, I didn't press her for more information. I hoped she'd tell me when she felt more comfortable.

We both looked towards the school building as the doors opened, and Mrs. Davies wheeled out a trolley that held a portable warm drinks dispenser and a silver plate covered in a cloche.

"Snack time!" she called out, and in the distance, I heard Coach Phillips blow his whistle to end the football game. "As a special reward for all your hard work this term, I arranged with the kitchen staff to have hot chocolate and cookies prepared."

The entire seventh grade class gathered around Mrs. Davies, as she filled disposable cups with thick, rich hot chocolate and added Cool Whip from a squirty can. Along with the cups of hot chocolate, she handed out festively decorated sugar cookies.

As Benjamin Franklin Academy was one of the best private schools in Boston, the hot chocolate and cookies were freshly made, rather than that of the instant variety, and both were full of flavor.

"Do you have anything left for me?" A male voice from behind asked.

I turned to see Coach Phillips standing just behind me, and my whole body flushed with heat. It didn't matter that Coach had to be at least twenty-years older than I was, I thought he was gorgeous. I'd never admit it out loud, but Coach Phillips had appeared in my dreams more than once. I'd even snuck into the school gymnasium and taken his picture down from the staff notice board. It was now hidden in an old shoe box under my bed, and I looked at it every night before going to sleep.

Read the complete story HERE!

SUBSCRIBE TO MY EXCLUSIVE NEWSLETTER

I hope you enjoyed reading this book.

If you want to stay updated on my upcoming releases, price promotions, and any ARC opportunities, then I would love to have you on my mailing list.

Subscribe yourself to my exclusive mailing list using the below link!

Subscribe to Lydia Hall's Exclusive Newsletter